No Time for Romance

Other Avalon Books by Lynne Loring

LOVE REMEMBERED

NO TIME FOR
Romance

LYNNE LORING

AVALON BOOKS
THOMAS BOUREGY AND COMPANY, INC.
401 LAFAYETTE STREET
NEW YORK, NEW YORK 10003

Fic
LOR
R

PRINTED IN THE UNITED STATES OF AMERICA
ON ACID-FREE PAPER
BY HADDON CRAFTSMEN, SCRANTON, PENNSYLVANIA

To the dedicated professionals who devote their
lives and their skill to the service of others

Chapter One

The man in the hospital bed stirred restlessly. A slight frown troubled his face, and he murmured fretfully in his sleep. He was young, perhaps in his early thirties, an athletic man with the deep tan and strong, muscular arms of a sportsman. Thick, glossy black hair curled appealingly across his brow; even the stubble of a day-old beard did not veil the handsome planes of his face. Nor did it hide the lines that creased the corners of his mouth and the heavy shadows beneath his eyes. Unwilling as he was to admit it, Tony Lawrence was in a great deal of pain.

Amanda Summers, a psychologist and counselor on the Social Services staff at City Medical Center, observed him silently from her position at the foot of his bed while she glanced over the patient profile detailed on the medical chart she held. Tony Lawrence was a familiar figure on the local sports page, as well known for his feats in race-car and polo circles as he was for the luxury hotel and several fine restaurants he operated in the city. Wealthy, handsome, socially prominent, he was remarkably successful for a man his age. He was also, at present, an extremely difficult patient.

Admitted to City Medical Center after a bad crash in a race-car competition, Tony had given the hospital staff nothing but trouble. The fact that he had suffered a fractured neck and for the first few days partial paralysis had failed to subdue him in the least. Although his doctors had explained to him that he faced a long period of rehabilitative therapy, it made no impression. He was uncooperative with the nursing staff, ignored his doctors' advice, and frustrated the members of his rehabilitation team with his refusal to cooperate. Tony was used to having his way, and he wanted no part of the hospital or treatment.

At last, Dr. Ian Foster, director of Rehabilitation Services, had asked Amanda, as the Social Services staff member assigned to Tony's rehab team, to see if she could get through to him. In the past, she had been successful with troublesome patients. Perhaps she could make Tony understand how important it was to follow the treatment program that had been prescribed for him.

The first step, of course, was getting him to accept the seriousness of his injury, Amanda speculated as she studied him thoughtfully. Seeing his features twist with pain as he tried to position his head more comfortably in his neck brace, she suspected that he knew full well how close he had come to disaster. But he wasn't yet ready to face the consequences of the accident. It was going to be very difficult for him to cope with the fact that his daredevil days were over.

She became aware then that his eyes were open and he was regarding her steadily. "Tony?" she said in a pleasant tone. "I'm Amanda Summers, from Social Services, and I've been assigned to your rehab team. I've come to see if there's anything I can do to help you."

His lips curved in a mocking smile, revealing even white teeth. "I can think of several things. That is, if we can figure out some way to get me out of this contraption they've got me trussed up in."

"I'm sure the brace is uncomfortable, but the important thing is that it's doing its work," she said crisply, ignoring his suggestive grin. "Why don't we see if we can't come up with some ways to help it along?"

He groaned. "I should have known it was too

good to be true. Here I wake up to find this gorgeous strawberry blonde standing at the foot of my bed, and I think that at last things are looking up for me. But now you tell me you've only come with more treatment.''

''I've come to talk to you about your treatment— or any other problems you may be having.''

His lip curled scornfully. ''Then you've got a tough job ahead of you.''

''Not necessarily. As a part of your treatment, the hospital provides a number of supporting services that can help you deal with your illness.''

''I'm not *ill*,'' he snapped.

''Incapacitated, then. At least temporarily.''

''Not from any of my doing. If I had my way, I'd be out of here today.''

''Of course you would. And soon you will be back at home. In the meantime, you can speed up your release by taking advantage of the services at the hospital. I'm here to explain them to you and try to answer any questions.''

''Now I see the pattern. Since the inquisition squad couldn't get the job done, they've sent a pretty one to work on me for a while.'' He managed a shrug and painfully tried to shift his position in bed. ''Well, gorgeous, I was never one to pass up a good thing. Let's talk.''

Amanda groaned inwardly. This was going to be even tougher than she had feared. It was her guess that behind his bravado, Tony was a very frightened man. And he had every reason to be, given his disheartening medical prognosis. The problem was going to be getting him to admit his fear and deal with it.

She moved to the side of the bed and got out the information form she was required to fill out. "I need to get some information from you, and then I'll try to answer any questions you may have. First, do you have any problems with finances or family that you need help with?"

He laughed sardonically. "If money would buy me a new neck, I'd already be out of here. As for family, I have none."

"No wife or parents?"

"No wife, no parents, no brothers or sisters."

"Any associates who are close to you?"

"If you're talking about a girlfriend, there's no one special. Would you be interested in the position?"

She ignored his remark. "I take it that you live alone. Will this be a problem when you're released from the hospital?"

"I have my houseman, Sam, to look after me."

"Good. We can arrange for him to get instructions in physical therapy and home care."

He tried to rise to a sitting position. "Stop right there. I'm perfectly capable of doing my own exercises, *if* I decide I need any, and I can certainly take care of myself—provided I get out of this chamber of horrors.''

''You mustn't exert yourself,'' Amanda cautioned, leaning over to settle her unruly patient. ''Please lie quietly while we talk. We'll accomplish much more if you can keep from getting upset.''

His hand closed around her wrist, and his lips curved into a mischievous grin. ''I'm not in the least upset, gorgeous. In fact, having you this close to me is the only good thing that has happened to me since I got here.''

The hand that gripped her wrist was surprisingly strong, and Amanda struggled for composure as she tried to free herself. ''Don't you think this is a bit childish?'' she asked coolly as she tried without success to pull her hand away. ''We can both make better use of our time.''

''I've got all the time in the world,'' he said, pulling her closer to him.

''But I don't. I think I can spend my time more usefully with another patient.'' Straightening, she waited for him to release her hand, coldly ignoring his provocative smile.

''Is there a problem here?'' a voice interrupted. A white-coated figure entered the room. Amanda looked up to meet the questioning gaze of a pair of ice-blue eyes. The gaze sharpened as the man standing in the doorway observed the scene. Striding toward the bed, followed by an assisting nurse, he admonished the patient sternly, "You know you're supposed to restrict your activity, Tony. Suppose you lie back as you've been instructed and let Miss"—his glance traveled to the identification badge pinned to Amanda's lab jacket—"Summers get on about her business while I take a look at you."

Amanda's spirits plummeted. Of all the people who could have walked in, Dr. Ross McKinnon was the absolute worst. Brusque, demanding, impatient on the best of occasions, he could be worse than caustic when confronted by unprofessional behavior. But, then, neurosurgeons tended to behave on a short string, their work being so sensitive.

Although he was the youngest and newest addition to the list of neurosurgeons at City Medical Center, Ross McKinnon was one of the best. His surgical skill had already won him the respect of his colleagues and the hospital staff. He was also as blunt with his patients as he was with staff, and he now regarded Tony with disapproval. His broad shoulders tensed with annoyance beneath his white lab coat as he ran an impatient hand through rumpled brown hair. Tony was not in the least intimidated, however. There was a challenge in his expression, and he didn't retreat before Ross's accusing stare.

Amanda took the opportunity to free her hand. Replacing the patient's chart in the holder at the foot of the bed, she turned to leave the room. "I'll come back later, Dr. McKinnon," she said as she passed him.

He gave her a curt nod of dismissal, and she hurried away, hoping that she didn't look as disconcerted as she felt. Outside in the corridor, she paused to gather her composure.

It was bad enough finding herself in such an awkward situation—one she should have been able to handle much more capably. Worse, though, was the fact that she had managed to present such a totally misleading picture of herself. This was her first assignment to one of Ross's patients, and she wanted to handle it well. Already he had shown impatience in dealing with the Social Services Department, and she disliked the thought that any action of hers might add to it. The department was always on trial with busy doctors who had a built-in intolerance for the volume of paperwork it required.

Resolved to guard against any more lapses, she turned her attention to the next patient she was scheduled to visit. She was glancing through the folder she carried, reviewing the details of the case, when she heard someone calling out to her. Looking up, she saw Ross was walking toward her. His expression warned that the incident with Tony Lawrence was not closed.

"I'd like a word with you," he said as he walked

up. "Apparently you're having some problems with Tony Lawrence."

"I'm sorry about the difficulty with him," Amanda said.

"Being sorry won't help him very much if he persists in the kind of activity I observed a moment ago. Surely you read his case history before you visited him."

"I read it very carefully."

"Then you don't need reminding how delicate his surgery was or how important this postoperative period is."

"Dr. Foster made his condition quite clear to me when he assigned me to the case. He also warned me that Tony is a difficult patient."

"Seriously injured people often are." The incisive blue eyes measured her critically. "If you don't think you can deal with Tony effectively, then maybe Dr. Foster ought to assign someone else to his case. Someone who would be less provocative," he added pointedly as his glance swept over her face, assessing the fluff of red-gold hair and her thickly lashed blue-green eyes.

Amanda suppressed her irritation. "I certainly didn't provoke the patient. He's feeling very threatened at the moment and was simply trying to assert his masculinity."

Ross leveled a frosty glance at her. "I studied psychology too. And I must say that we're serving our patient very poorly if all we can offer is a pretty therapist for him to flirt with. We'll do a far better job of reinforcing his masculinity by helping him make as complete a recovery as possible. Do you agree?''

"Of course. And I assure you I was entirely professional in my dealings with the patient. I'm used to handling such situations.''

He paused for a candid assessment of her trim figure and evenly proportioned features. "I bet you are. Dr. Foster probably took that factor into consideration when he assigned you to the case. Maybe he thought you could supply some incentive that the rest of us haven't come up with.'' A sudden, dry smile played around his mouth and the corners of his eyes crinkled attractively. "I just hope the patient is ready to handle so much incentive.''

Amanda met his inspection steadfastly. "If I had the slightest question about my effectiveness with any patient, I'd be the first to report it,'' she said.

"I'd certainly hope so. In any event, go ahead and see what you can do with Tony, but I'll have to reserve judgment until I see how he responds to you.''

With a quick nod, he strode off down the hall to join the nurse who stood waiting for him outside a patient's door. As Amanda watched his tall, rangy figure disappear into the room, she battled her bruised professional dignity. Ross McKinnon wasn't the first arrogant doctor she'd had to deal with, but he was surely one of the most upsetting. It was totally unfair of him to jump to conclusions about her professional conduct without giving her the slightest chance to justify herself.

Her thoughts were troubled as she went on to her next assignment. In the brief time she had spent with him, she had found out that Tony Lawrence was a complicated case. It was going to take all the rehab team's skills to treat him successfully, and alienating his physician wouldn't make the work any easier. If Ross was convinced that she was a featherbrained incompetent, she would only be a hindrance to the team.

By the time she finished her morning schedule, Amanda had made a decision. She intended to meet her problems with Ross head-on. The best thing to do would be to report his dissatisfaction to Dr. Foster, head of the rehab team, explain the unfortunate incident, and seek his advice.

Dr. Ian Foster was a man in his late fifties with a shock of iron-gray hair and an engaging smile. He ran the rehab department with compassion for patients balanced with a dispassionate approach to their needs. Unfortunately, what patients wanted wasn't always the best treatment for them.

Each case was handled by a team of medical specialists supervised by Dr. Foster. The team was made up of the various therapists whose services were required, along with the nursing supervisor in the rehab section and a counselor from Social Services. As the counselor assigned to the case, Amanda was responsible for evaluating the patient and obtaining any help from the Social Services Department the patient might need. In consultation with the prescribing physician, Dr. Foster decided on the treatment program and coordinated the efforts of the team.

Amanda was frequently assigned to Dr. Foster's rehab teams. She found him to be a perceptive and understanding adviser and held the greatest respect for him. He, in turn, always seemed satisfied with her work.

She found him in his office, thumbing through a tall stack of patient folders. At her tentative rap on his door, he looked up and smiled. "I've been expecting you, Amanda."

She slipped dejectedly into a chair. "You've already heard."

"Ross McKinnon paid me a visit a little while ago. Apparently you've made quite an impression on him."

"Not quite the one I'd have liked. He came into Tony Lawrence's room at precisely the wrong moment. A minute later and I would have had things under control."

Dr. Foster chuckled. "I'm afraid Ross doesn't

have the greatest understanding of these things. Somehow patients don't give their surgeons the same hard time they give their therapists.''

''I can't imagine anybody giving Ross Mc-Kinnon a hard time,'' Amanda said grudgingly.

''He would ignore it if they did. You have to realize that Ross can't afford a lot of sentiment in the work he does. His patients usually have very serious problems, and he doesn't often have many options to choose from. He can't let compassion influence his decisions.''

''He made that very clear to me. The thing is, he jumped to the wrong conclusion about Tony and wouldn't let me explain.''

Dr. Foster's professional interest sharpened. ''Tell me about Tony. What were you able to find out?''

''Not too much, unfortunately. He hasn't yet accepted the seriousness of his injury, of course, and he has some obvious psychological problems to work through before he's going to respond to his therapy. I was just beginning to get some response from him when Dr. McKinnon came in . . .''

''. . . and misunderstood the response,'' Dr. Foster finished for her. ''All he saw was a pretty woman and an overstimulated patient.''

''He's convinced I'm some kind of an airhead paper-pusher who hasn't any better sense than to make a move on a patient,'' Amanda said disgustedly.

"Ross has little understanding of the support services at the hospital. He recognizes the need for therapy but in the busy press of his schedule hasn't the time to acquaint himself with its demands. You have to remember that he couldn't do his work if he were bogged down in the details of ours. Try to be patient with him. It's up to us to prove ourselves.''

"I certainly hope to, provided he doesn't bump me from the team. And I'd very much like to work on this case, Dr. Foster. I think Tony is a troubled man, and our problem will be getting him to accept our help.''

"I agree. The members of the team will just have to keep trying to get through to him.''

"Does that include me?'' Amanda asked with a wry smile.

"At least for the time being. Do what you can with him between now and our staff meeting on Friday. Perhaps we can give Ross a report that will reassure him. You understand, of course, that if he asks me to remove you from the team, I'll have to honor his request.''

She sighed. "I know.''

"Then do the best you can,'' he said with an understanding smile. "Good luck, Amanda.''

She left his office, deploring the unfortunate position in which she found herself. How could she possibly have managed to get off to such an abysmal start with the testy Dr. Ross McKinnon?

But then, as she reviewed their conversation, a small ray of hope flickered. Maybe the impression she had made wasn't totally negative. She had at least attracted some small notice. She would simply have to show him there was more to her than a pleasing face and an empty head.

It was up to her to prove to Ross that he was wrong about her. She had to convince him that the service she offered was necessary and that she was entirely capable of performing it effectively. The best way to show him would be to succeed with his patient.

Chapter Two

Amanda's campaign to prove herself to Dr. Ross McKinnon was even more difficult than she had imagined. Knowing his doubts about her capability, she became acutely conscious of him. Before her unhappy encounter with him in Tony's room, he was just another name on the list of doctors. Now she seemed to run into him at every turn.

No matter how she timed them, her visits to patients coincided with his hospital rounds. He turned up in areas of the hospital where she had never seen him before—his tall, imposing figure appearing in the corridors at the most unexpected times. One morning in the physical therapy department, he walked in while she was sitting beside a patient who was painfully doing push-ups on a floor mat while they discussed the arrangements she had made for home therapy. She ran into him again in the surgical wing as she was taking an elderly man for an exhilarating ride in a wheelchair while they talked about the patient's transfer to a convalescent center. Wherever she went, Ross seemed to be there too.

Not that she wanted to hide from him. It was just that she wanted to delay any confrontation until after she had dealt successfully with Tony. Unfortunately, that goal was turning out to be an elusive one. Tony continued to be difficult, shutting out therapists and staff alike and resisting their efforts to help. He refused to deal with the fact that he had suffered a serious injury, and he approached his treatment with cynical disdain. In short, he was a pain in the neck.

In view of their lack of success, Amanda hoped to delay an accounting to Ross as long as possible. She tried to avoid him as best she could, ducking into doorways when she spied him approaching or passing him with a quick nod and hurrying on her way. Still, she couldn't help but notice his doubtful expression and the quizzical way he looked at her. She knew that she was only putting off the moment when she would have to face his skepticism.

It came one morning in the pediatric wing. She had stopped in to visit a young patient whose mother had requested help from the Social Services

Department. The boy, a disarming four-year-old who had undergone corrective orthopedic surgery, was being sent to a children's facility for further treatment. Amanda was assembling the data required to obtain the financial assistance that his mother needed for his care.

She had turned into the doorway of his room when a ball rolled across the floor into her path. Retrieving the ball, she returned it to the young patient, who sat in the bed, eyeing her mischievously. When he bounced the ball to her, she tossed it back to him. "I see you're ready to play," she said, smiling at him.

He eagerly returned the ball, and a game of catch followed, ending only when Amanda failed to catch the ball and it rolled under the bed. The boy laughed with delight while he watched her crawl under the bed to retrieve it.

She was backing out from her cramped position when she became aware of a pair of long legs silhouetted in the doorway of the room. Looking up, she met Ross's curious gaze. He was lounging against the door, watching her. Embarrassed to have been caught in such an unprofessional posture, she struggled to her feet, handed the ball to the boy, and mumbled a hasty greeting to the puzzled doctor as she retreated unceremoniously from the room.

To her dismay, he intercepted her outside the

door, blocking her path as she tried to hurry off down the hall. Having no choice but to stop, she waited apprehensively as he looked down at her with a questioning expression in his eyes. "Tell me," he said. "Am I somehow out of touch, or are you a bit unorthodox in your approach to your work?"

"I don't know," Amanda stammered, pressed for a suitable answer.

He considered her thoughtfully. "Does it ever seem to you that you go about things a bit differently?"

Confused, she could only shrug. "I just try to relate to my patients as best I can."

"I've noticed," he said. After a moment's inspection, he turned away.

Amanda exhaled with relief as he set off down the hall. What an unpredictable man. A person could never tell what he was thinking—or when he was going to appear. Unhappily, too, she still had to deal with Tony, whom she had not yet visited again. Although she had been instructed by Dr. Foster to continue her evaluation of Tony's progress, she had deliberatedly delayed a meeting with him. She wanted to give Tony time to mend physically as well as emotionally.

The visit could be postponed no longer, however, and she had scheduled it for later on in the day. A staff conference was being held late that

afternoon, at which time she would be expect[
deliver a report.

She sighed at the prospect. Between her trou
blesome patient and a skeptical doctor, she had her
work cut out for her.

Amanda entered Tony's hospital room, fortified
against another difficult encounter. Now forewarned, she was prepared to ward off any more
amorous overtures. She had only to keep in mind
that he was a seriously injured man who was trying
to deny his fears.

She found him in subdued spirits, however. He
lay quietly in bed, his eyes fixed on the limited
view from his hospital window. At first, he seemed
unaware of her presence. Only when she stood at
the foot of his bed did he rouse from his reverie.
A feeble smile curved his lips when he recognized
her, but he made no attempt to straighten up in the
bed. ''I see they've decided to try the pretty one
again. They must be near the end of their string,''
he said.

''Not at all. We're only beginning. Now that
you've had time to think about it, I've come back
to find out how we can help you,'' she said with
a professional smile. As she evaluated her listless
patient, she decided that Tony was a discouraged
man. Apparently he'd accepted the fact that he
couldn't bluster his injury away.

arily. "I doubt that there's

—unless you can get me

ng, Tony. When you're ready,

ed and so busy you'll be begging

rest."

from what? Weaving baskets?" he said

ly. "Forget it. I'm not into arts and crafts."

You'll have to take that up with your occupational therapist. That's not my department. I'm
here on another matter. I need to talk to you about
what to do when it's time for you to go home."

A faint hope flickered in his eyes. "Are they
going to release me?"

"Not until you've recovered from your surgery.
In the meantime, we need to make arrangements
for your home care after you leave the hospital. A
lot will depend on your progress in therapy, of
course, but we need to think about how you'll manage." She looked at the clipboard she carried. "I
believe you said you live alone but have someone
to look after you."

"Sam runs the house and takes care of things
for me. I won't have any trouble there."

"How about your work? Will it be a problem if
you have to take a little time to ease back into it?"

"Work isn't a problem. I have people who are
perfectly capable of doing what needs to be done.

If there's anything that needs my attention, they'll bring it to me.''

Amanda noticed his lack of interest. She decided to probe a little further into his state of mind. ''Will transportation be a problem? You may not be driving right away.''

She watched him closely. His answer to her question would be significant. Tony had rolled a high-speed race car three times and was lucky to be alive. She had also learned that this was the first really serious crash he had experienced. It wouldn't be surprising if he never wanted to sit at the wheel of a car again.

Her question didn't seem to provoke any particular reaction, however. ''Sam will drive me wherever I want to go,'' he said.

''You're very fortunate, Tony. There don't seem to be any obstacles to your going home, so it will be easier for your therapists to determine the best treatment program for you. You should be able to move right along with your rehabilitation.'' She closed the cover of her clipboard. ''Of course, you can call on us if you need anything. We're here to help you in any way we can.''

His lips curved in any ironic smile. ''You recited that speech very well. I'll report to Dr. McKinnon that you performed very professionally. You got through the transportation bit without a slipup, and you didn't ask a single question about how I'm reacting to having nearly killed myself. I thought you'd surely offer to detraumatize me.''

''Do you need to be detraumatized?''

''If you're asking if I'm afraid to climb back into a race car, the answer is no,'' he said with a trace of defiance. ''When you decide to race a car, you know there's always the chance of an accident. It's a risk you have to take.''

''And I take it that the risk has never bothered you.''

He shifted irritably. ''Of course not. I wouldn't have raced if it did. The risk is part of the challenge.''

''I see.'' She let the subject drop. She had uncovered the clue she had been seeking.

She spent another moment or two talking to Tony about inconsequential matters. When she did not pursue the subject of racing, Tony seemed to retreat into reticence. When she turned to leave, he made only a fainthearted effort at banter. ''In case you don't get back to me, I'll try to think up something I need. You're the only attraction in this place.''

''I'm sure there are plenty of attractions waiting for you at home.''

''I wish there were.'' There was a hint of dejection in the dark eyes, but his lips curved into a smile. ''Unless, of course, you'd like to drop by and keep me company.''

Amanda laughed. "Once you leave here, you'll never want to see me again."

"I don't think so," he said.

Ignoring the suggestion, she went on to her next assignment, pensively considering the information she had gleaned. She may have discovered the key to understanding Tony Lawrence. The question now was how best to use that knowledge.

The staff meeting that afternoon started late. As happened frequently, Dr. Foster was delayed. The other members of the rehabilitation team drifted into the meeting room one by one. "What a day," Connie D'Angelo exclaimed as she plopped into a chair next to Amanda. "My patients are ready for a weekend off, and so am I."

Connie was the physical therapist assigned to Tony's rehab team. She was also Amanda's roommate. They had met through work and struck up a congenial friendship that had led to their decision to share an apartment. A vivacious young woman with dark, short-cropped hair, lively brown eyes, and a happy disposition, Connie usually bubbled with enthusiasm. Today she slumped in her chair and sighed. "I don't know about you, but I could use some R & R. Would you like to stop off after work for a pizza and maybe take in a movie?"

"I'd love it," Amanda answered. "Especially

the movie. Maybe we could find one about romantic people and undying love.''

''More likely it will be a choice between a serial killer and a villain blowing away half the East Coast, but I'm game if you are.''

''Whatever. Just so it's fun.''

Connie glanced at Amanda questioningly. ''I see you've had one of those days too. I hope you haven't had another run-in with Ross McKinnon.''

''I haven't seen him at all. Boy, news certainly travels fast in this place. Has everybody in the hospital heard about him dressing me down?'' Amanda asked, chagrined.

''Just about. The nurse overheard it.''

''And talked,'' Amanda said disgustedly. ''How professional of her.''

''Actually, she thought you stood up to him rather well.''

''I may not be standing up for very long. It all depends on what he does after this staff meeting. He may decide he doesn't want me on Tony's rehab team.''

''We all may be off the case if Tony continues to be difficult to work with. Frankly, I'm still getting nowhere with him.'' Connie's voice dropped to a whisper as Dr. Foster entered the room, signaling the start of the staff meeting. ''Let's hope Dr. Foster has got some ideas.''

The first cases the team reviewed presented no

problems and were finished promptly, leaving the rest of the time for discussion of Tony's case. Each member of the team reported on his progress. In each case, the results were disheartening. Tony was still not responding to his therapists; he was still uncooperative. The only good news was that his recovery from surgery was progressing satisfactorily.

Amanda's report was the last called for. She had listened, discouraged, to the other members of the team, feeling that she had little to add to the profile that had emerged.

"There really doesn't seem to be much that Social Services can do for Tony," she began. "He has no financial problems, and his physical needs will be taken care of once he leaves. The only help he seems to need is medical. Except. . . ." She hesitated.

"If you have any thoughts, we want to hear them," Dr. Foster prompted.

"I may be quite mistaken, of course," Amanda continued, "but from my conversations with Tony, I picked up on some feelings that might be useful to us. For a man as successful as he is, he has surprisingly little interest in his business affairs. There also seems to be little of importance to him in his personal life—no special friends."

"I'm not sure the nurses would agree," Ann Smythe, the nursing supervisor, objected. "They

said his room was like a country club when he came
down from ICU. They had to shoo people out and
put a limit on visitors.''

''That was true for the first day or so,'' Amanda
pointed out. ''But when I checked, I discovered
that he's had very few visitors since.''

''His friend Sam is here every day.''

''Sam is his houseman. He's the only person
Tony speaks of, and there has been no woman
mentioned at all. I think it's odd. A handsome,
successful man with Tony's appeal ought to have
a woman in his life who cares about him.'' Amanda
shook her head. ''I think we're dealing with a
lonely man who has nothing special in his life except his daring exploits. The risk-taking gives him
incentive.''

''If that's the case, he's going to have to find
another incentive,'' a voice spoke up from the back
of the room. Amanda turned to see Ross leaning
against the wall just inside the door. Apparently,
he had entered the room sometime during their
discussion.

''As a surgeon, I can't do any more for this
patient,'' he said. ''His injury is in a vulnerable
area, and he's got to avoid any reinjury. The surgery we did was very risky, and the chances of
repeating it successfully are poor. The degree to
which he recovers from this accident is going to
depend on what he can do through rehabilitative

therapy. And, of course, he'll need to limit himself to sensible physical activity. I'm afraid Tony has no choice but to accept his limitations. One way or another, his daredevil days are over.''

''Then our job will be to convince him of this and help him understand the importance of his therapy,'' Dr. Foster said. ''Since we've had no success so far, does anyone have any ideas?''

There was a discouraging silence.

''Amanda might try to get through to him,'' Ross suggested. ''So far, she's about the only one of us who seems to have gotten any response from him. Maybe she can find a way to convince him that he really hasn't any option but to cooperate.''

''He's a very strong-willed man, which at present is working to his disadvantage. Our task is to get him to direct his willfulness toward his treatment,'' Dr. Foster pointed out. He turned to Amanda. ''Keep on trying and see if you can build a rapport with him. Maybe you'll have a breakthrough.''

Amanda left the meeting feeling encouraged. At least she was still on Tony's rehab team. And she was confident that she'd be able to help him, given time. She was convinced that Tony's resistance to his treatment was simply his way of refusing to face reality. If they could help him redirect his feelings, they could set him on the path to recovery.

She left Connie with a promise to meet her after

work and started back to her office. Halfway down the hall, a lanky figure fell in beside her. It was Ross. "I was interested in your comments about Tony. If you have time for a cup of coffee, I'd like to talk to you about him."

Surprised, Amanda agreed. While she was encouraged by his approving attitude, she followed him warily to the staff lounge near the nurses' station on the floor. He poured two cups of coffee and sat down beside her on the utilitarian sofa that offered the most comfortable seating in the room. Taking a sip of coffee, he grimaced at its bitter taste. "Hospital coffee is surely the worst in the world. Who do you suppose brews this stuff?" he asked.

"I think it only comes in industrial strength," Amanda said lightly. "It is pretty awful, isn't it?"

"Maybe it's intended to jolt you into action." He set down the Styrofoam cup. "I didn't ask you here to talk about the coffee, though. I wanted to know how you came up with your analysis of Tony. Apparently, you've been able to get close to him."

There was a hint in his words that Amanda wanted to dispel at once. "It wasn't my objective to get close to him. Because of the nature of my work, though, I do ask patients many questions. In Tony's case, his answers turned out to be revealing. Apparently, he loves the risk involved in feats of daring. Without the hope of returning to them, he lacks the motivation for a successful re-habilitation. Of course, I may be completely wrong.''

''I don't think so,'' Ross said, his expression somber. ''I think you've pegged him just right. And if you have, Tony could be in trouble. He has to face some real changes in his life-style. If he can't find his motivation in ordinary pursuits, he's in for a major disappointment.''

''What if he refuses to give up racing?''

''Then he could be looking at some heavy con-sequences. Reinjury to his spine could result in total paralysis if it didn't kill him. But the choice is his. I've done all I can for him with surgery, and I've explained his options to him. If he chooses to ignore our advice, there's nothing we can do about it.''

Amanda shook her head regretfully. ''I just can't help feeling sorry for him. He seems like such a lonely man. He says he has no family, no wife, not even an important woman in his life. And I have to wonder why. He's an exceptionally attrac-tive person, and he's obviously an astute busi-nessman. Why wouldn't he be brimming over with enthusiasm for life?''

Ross shrugged. ''There's no explaining people. You have to deal with them the way they are.''

''But if you can understand them, it makes deal-ing with them so much easier. I did some reading up on Tony and discovered that he has been responsible for his family business since he was in his early twenties. According to the stories I read, his father suffered from a long, debilitating illness, and it was up to Tony to look after him and hold things together. After his father's death Tony got into auto racing, polo playing, speedboats, motorcycles, and all. It would be interesting to know what prompted him to turn in that direction.''

''You've developed quite a fascination for Tony, haven't you?'' Ross said, regarding her with interest.

''As a patient, yes. I can't help wondering why he's so alone.''

''Maybe he's given people good reason to leave him alone. He might not be the world's most likable guy.''

''Not according to the newspaper articles I read. The stories about him all describe him as being surrounded by friends. I keep thinking that if we don't care about Tony, who will?''

He seemed surprised by her intensity. ''Of course we care about him. We're in this business to help people. But our job is to offer people the best health care we can, not to try to manage their lives for them. We can't take on their problems. In Tony's case, he's got some hard decisions to make.''

''But surely we owe it to him to help him make the best decision,'' Amanda insisted.

"We can give him the facts as we see them, but it's up to him to deal with them."

"What if he can't deal with them?"

"He has to, one way or another. We do our part, he does his. That's the way it has to be." His expression softened as he added, "Look on the bright side, Amanda. We've patched him up, he's healed very well, and before too long I'll be able to release him. Tony is a lucky man. It could just as easily have gone the other way."

Encouraged by Ross's candid manner, Amanda ventured a final remark. "I just wish Tony could see how fortunate he is and what he could accomplish if he would cooperate."

Ross rose from the sofa, walked to the metal sink at the end of the room, and poured his untouched coffee down the drain. "I have a feeling Tony is a lost cause. He's going to do what he wants to do in spite of you or me or anybody else."

"Maybe so, but I'd like to keep on trying."

"Then I wish you success in your crusade, but I've got a long list of other, more cooperative patients whom I need to see." He ambled toward the door, calling back over his shoulder, "Don't care too much. You'll burn yourself out. And, unorthodox as your methods may be, we can't have you doing that. There are too many other people who need you." With a nonchalant wave he set off down the hall.

Amanda stood for a time in the doorway looking after him. It occurred to her, as she watched him, that he had insulated himself with a protective shell, setting himself apart from the illness and disease he dealt with daily. Yet she wondered if perhaps he cared more than he professed. No doctor could be as dedicated as he was without having real compassion for people.

Suddenly she was very curious about Ross McKinnon. She couldn't help but wonder what kind of man he was away from the hospital. Did he have a family? A wife? Some woman he loved?

But why was *she* so curious? What Ross did in his personal life was his own business. His attachments, whatever they were, were no concern of hers.

Chapter Three

For the next several days, Amanda was caught up in her busy schedule. The caseload in Social Services was always heavy, and there were never enough hours in the day. It was late in the week before she saw Tony again.

She had stopped by Physical Therapy at Connie's request. A patient of Connie's, an elderly woman who was recovering from a broken hip, was being released from the hospital but would need continued physical therapy at home. The Social Services Department had been asked to arrange funding for a visiting therapist, and Amanda was setting up the service. She had obtained the information she needed and was passing through the treatment area when someone called out to her. She recognized

Tony. He wore a neck brace and walked stiffly, but he was moving freely.

"It's good to see you out and around," she said as he reached her side. "Are you feeling better?"

"I'm getting there. They let me out of my room now, but there isn't much happening outside to interest me. As a matter of fact, I've been wondering where they were hiding you. It's dull around here without you."

"I wouldn't say that." Amanda looked around the large room where patients and therapists were hard at work. Some patients lay on exercise tables, others worked on mats or in the walking bars, all of them patiently retraining damaged muscles and coaxing injured bodies to perform. "I see some very exciting things going on in here."

"I guess it's all in your point of view. To me, it's just going through the same boring motions over and over."

"The repetition is what makes the therapy work. It's hard to tell that you're making any progress, but gradually you get there. It just takes patience. Physical therapy isn't a lot different from an athletic workout, you know. Being the athlete you are, I should think that you'd take quite well to it."

"I've done weight training, and as soon as I get home, I'll do it again."

"I'm glad to hear you say that. That kind of attitude will help you recover."

"Are you trying to challenge me?" he asked with a cynical glance.

She smiled. "As a matter of fact, I am. That's my job."

"And here I thought you were doing all this for me because you and I had something special. I had great plans for us, and now I find I'm just another statistic to you."

There was a challenge in his teasing words that Amanda studiedly ignored. "Not at all. You're a patient with very real needs, and I want to help you in any way I can."

"I can think of a number of ways you could help," he said slyly. "For starters, you might consider coming around to keep me company when I get home. I've gotten word that my doctor is getting ready to boot me out of here any day now."

"Then you must be coming along very well."

"And you've very neatly sidestepped my invitation." He looked at her expectantly, clearly not intending to be put off. She was saved an answer when Connie came toward them.

"Hi, Amanda. Did you get the information you needed on my patient?" she called out.

Amanda patted the clipboard she carried. "It's all right here. By the time she gets home, I'll have a schedule worked out for her."

Connie nodded. "I knew I could count on you to grease the wheels. We didn't get much notice that she was being discharged.'' She turned her attention to Tony. ''And speaking of being discharged, you're just the man I'm looking for. I'm going to help you develop a home rehab program. I can arrange for Sam to come in for instruction if you like.''

Tony brushed aside the offer. ''Not necessary. Sam is a seasoned trainer. He's been helping me keep in shape for years.''

''These aren't ordinary workout exercises, Tony,'' Connie warned. ''They're very specifically designed, and there's a sequence to them. You'll still need to come to the hospital for supervision on a regular basis. We have to make sure you're ready before we move you through the levels of therapy, and Dr. McKinnon will have to approve.''

''If you say so, but there's no need to involve Sam. I can tell him what we're supposed to do.'' He turned to Amanda. ''Incidentally, I want you to know that I've turned over a new leaf. I promise to do as I'm told. That seems to be my ticket to getting out of here.''

''Your *improvement* will be your ticket out of here,'' Amanda said.

''Don't I at least rate some good-conduct points with you?'' Tony feigned disappointment. ''After all, I'm doing all this to impress you.''

''Do it for yourself,'' Amanda replied.

"But surely I can hope for a bonus," he persisted.

"Whatever works for you," Connie intervened. "Right now we need to get on with the show." Taking Tony by the arm, she steered him toward the treatment area to begin his therapy session.

Amanda turned away, feeling a twinge of doubt. Tony might be taking a more constructive approach to his therapy, but he was doing it for entirely the wrong reason. He couldn't look to someone else to supply him with a motive. It had to come from within.

The rest of the day was crowded with appointments that brought patients with new needs and additional requests for services. Amanda was kept busy gathering information and dealing with documentation. She was alone in the office she shared with two other counselors when, well into the afternoon, a woman hurried through the door and approached her desk.

"They said at the nurses' station I should come here," the woman began in obvious agitation. "They said there's nothing they can do for my husband upstairs until the papers from the doctor come through."

"Tell me what the problem is, and I'll see if I can help." Amanda motioned to the chair beside her desk, hoping to calm her visitor.

The woman refused the chair and stood anxiously in front of Amanda's desk. "My husband is due for release tomorrow and was scheduled to be transferred to a nursing center, but the center says they can't accept him without proper authorization from his doctor. They say they can't hold a place for him past tomorrow, and I just don't know what I'll do if I can't work this out. There's no way I can take care of him at home by myself."

"Did Social Services make the arrangements for you?" Amanda asked.

"They had it all worked out, and I thought everything was in order until I went to the nursing center today to finalize the arrangements. That's when we found out the papers weren't there. I've been trying all day to get through to the doctor, but the people at his office say he can't be reached."

Amanda calmed the woman as best she could and quickly gathered the information she needed to check on the case. Examining the records, she learned that the patient had undergone surgery for an aneurysm and required temporary treatment in a special nursing facility. Such facilities were hard to find at any time. Apparently, a suitable place had been found for him, but it had to be accepted at once or lost.

Observing the patient's wife, Amanda could see at once that she was not exaggerating her predicament. A frail woman who appeared to be in her mid-sixties, she was clearly unequal to the physical task of caring for a semi-invalid. It was imperative that the doctor on the case be contacted at once.

"I'll get busy on this right away," she promised. "As soon as I find out what's holding up the paperwork, I'll get back in touch with you."

As the distressed woman left the office to return to her husband's hospital room, Amanda scanned the patient's records and found that Ross was his physician. Of the many doctors the department dealt with, he was surely one of the most difficult to track down.

A call to his office determined that the papers Amanda sought were still on his desk, unsigned. His assistant, Laurie Collins, told her that he was in emergency surgery and had been unavailable all day. She couldn't say when he would be free.

Amanda understood the demands on the neurosurgeons, who bore a heavy share of the hospital's emergencies, but the needs of a patient and his family were important too. A call to the nursing center determined that they were caught in the crush of short supply and heavy demand for space and could hold a room for the patient only if the required paperwork had been completed. Since immediate action was needed, Amanda decided to get the forms from Ross's office, take them to the surgical floor, and wait until she could get him to sign them.

At the nurses' station on the surgical floor, she

found out that Ross was still in surgery but would be finished soon. Leaving word for him at the desk, she settled in to wait. She would put the time to good use by reading the stack of reports she had brought from her office.

She had almost finished her reading when he came out of surgery, looking distracted and a bit impatient, still wearing blue surgical scrubs. She jumped to her feet and hurried to intercept him. "I know you're very busy, and I'm sorry to bother you, but I need your signature on these papers," she explained quickly, indicating the forms she carried. "I wouldn't ask if it weren't important."

"I'm sure it is or you wouldn't be here," he said, reaching for the papers. As he glanced over them, a slight frown crossed his face. "Right now, I'm on my way to check on a patient who's in recovery. But if you can hang around for a few minutes, I'll take care of these. I like to read what I'm signing."

"Of course. I'll wait here," she said as he returned the papers to her.

With an abrupt nod, he strode off down the hallway toward the recovery rooms.

She sat down and resumed her reading, prepared for another long wait. Instead, he reappeared a short time later, dropping into the chair beside her with a weary sigh. "I can take a look at those papers now," he said, running a hand through his tousled brown hair. He stretched his long legs out in front of him and slid down in the chair as he read.

When he had finished, he reached for the pen Amanda extended to him and scrawled an unreadable signature on the papers. ''My patient was waiting for these, wasn't he?'' he said as he handed them back to her. ''I'm sorry they got mishandled, but it has been really busy around here. There seems to have been a demolition derby on the freeway, and several short-tempered folks decided to shoot each other. We've just got our last patient stabilized.''

Amanda stole a glance at him, noting the fatigue around his eyes and the light shadow of beard on his chin. He was clearly a weary man. Seeing him in wrinkled scrubs in the arena where he worked, she gained a renewed appreciation of how important his job was.

''I apologize for hitting you with paperwork when you're involved in such serious emergencies. You must be exhausted,'' she said.

''Other patients have problems too, that can get overlooked. It's a good thing they've got somebody to look after them.'' He looked at her questioningly. ''Will my patient get the service he needs now?''

''Oh, yes. I'll get in touch with the nursing center and arrange for the paperwork to be sent along with him when he transfers to the center tomorrow.''

Ross nodded. "Then he should be all right. With good care and followup therapy, he'll make a satisfactory recovery."

"In which case, I'd better go give his wife the good news. I'm sure you'd like to get back to work." She gathered her papers, preparing to leave.

He made no effort to rise from his chair, instead eyeing her tentatively. "As a matter of fact," he said after a moment, "I'm off duty for a while. It just occurred to me that I haven't had lunch and it's almost time to begin thinking about dinner. Would you be interested in joining me for a totally indigestible supper at the diner across the street? Maybe we could talk about our paperwork problems and see if we can't improve our lines of communication. Our patients seem to be getting lost in the system."

"I'd like that. I have some ideas about how we might simplify our procedures," Amanda said.

"Then why don't you finish up your work while I run a last check on my patients and get changed? We could meet at the ground-floor elevators." When Amanda agreed, he dragged himself reluctantly to his feet. "The food isn't much at the diner, but it's close to the hospital. At this point I'm willing to settle for someplace to sit down."

As Amanda hurried off to complete her tasks, she decided that there was another side to Ross.

Maybe he wasn't quite the demanding, autocratic doctor he seemed. Seeing him in the tense atmosphere of the surgery, she had a fuller understanding of the constant demands upon his time and skill. In fact, considering those demands, Ross had no business at all eating the infamous food at the diner across the street. He needed a nutritious, properly prepared meal. She knew exactly where he could get it too, if he was willing to consider her suggestion.

An hour later, Amanda was seated opposite Ross in a comfortably cushioned booth at Kovac's, a favorite eating place that she and Connie had discovered. Tucked away in a side street near the hospital, it was clean, comfortable, and quiet. Attractively decorated with green plants and yellow-checked tablecloths, it offered a restful atmosphere and featured delicious soups, salads, and home-cooked dinners personally prepared by the energetic owner, Sophie Kovac.

"This definitely beats the diner," Ross said as he glanced around him approvingly. "I never knew this place was here."

"Sophie opened it last year. She used to work in the hospital cafeteria, and she always wanted to run a restaurant of her own. When she got the chance to lease this place, she jumped at it. She cooks all the food herself and is very health-conscious about what she serves. Sophie's convinced that hospital workers have the unhealthiest diets of anybody.''

''She's right about that. Most of them are too busy to think about what they eat.'' His face brightened as he looked over the menu. ''I haven't eaten chicken and dumplings in years. Are the dumplings good?''

''Like a feather,'' Amanda promised. ''And the vegetables Sophie serves are perfect.''

When their food arrived, Ross attacked it heartily, pronouncing it to be all that she had promised. When he had finished, he leaned back in his chair, contented. With a pager attached to his belt, he could relax and give his attention to the problem that had brought them here.

''I'm sorry about the unsigned papers,'' he said. ''I don't want you to think I'm insensitive to the practical problems of my patients. It's just that, for me, paperwork has to be done on a catch-as-catch-can basis. My schedule isn't predictable.''

''You can't dictate emergencies,'' Amanda agreed. ''Social Services has them too. We have to coordinate a lot of things, and sometimes we have to act fast to get what the patient needs. Dealing with so many different agencies involves a volume of paperwork that we know is annoying to the doctors, but there's only so much we can do. We honestly try to accommodate your schedules as best we can, but sometimes doctors get squeezed. We're perfectly willing to streamline the process to fit the individual doctor, of course. Just let us know how you want us to contact you, and we'll do it.''

''I thought it worked pretty well today, although I don't see you having a lot of time to hang out at surgery,'' he said with a grin.

She returned his smile. ''Most of the surgeons wouldn't like it anyway. They would object to being disturbed at such a busy time.''

''Then let them come up with their own solutions. Me, I liked seeing you there. I don't suppose that's quite what you're looking for, however. If you'll put a note on any papers you send me, with the date by which the papers need to be returned, my assistant will see that I get them back to you on time. Of course, that might mean you would have to catch up with me occasionally, but I take it that you wouldn't mind.''

''Absolutely not. I want to work with you in any way I can, and I'm sure the other counselors in Social Services feel the same way. We just want to do the best job we can for the patients and be helpful to the doctors.''

''You certainly go out of your way to be helpful—if your dinner recommendation is an example.'' Ross glanced around the dining room while he took a sip of tea. ''This place is a find. It may turn out to be my ticket to survival.''

"I'm glad you like it. I hate to think of you settling for a heavy, greasy sandwich after your long day in surgery."

"You know, of course, that you're a born caretaker, don't you?" he asked, appraising her over the rim of his mug. "You always seem to be looking after people."

"Only if I can help them. But I'm not a meddler," Amanda added hastily.

"Far from it. People are lucky if there's someone around who's willing to take that extra step for them." He turned his mug slowly between the palms of his hands as he regarded her for a long moment. "I'm glad to be one of the people on your list."

Amanda was inordinately pleased by his approval. When he was paged a short time later and had to return to the hospital, she was disappointed that their dinner had come to an end.

They walked back to the hospital together, continuing a companionable conversation. He took time to accompany her to the hospital parking lot and waited until she was safely locked into her car. "Thanks for dinner," he said before he left her. "You've got a way of brightening things up for a guy."

With a quick smile and a wave, he turned away and headed toward the emergency-room entrance to the hospital. Amanda drove home, contented.

She decided that maybe Ross wasn't nearly as impassive about people as he might seem. Behind his shell of detachment, there was a doctor with real concern for his patients and a man with real regard for people.

Chapter Four

It was one of the rare weeks in the Social Services Department when the work moved along smoothly, there were no crises to deal with, and both patients and doctors had no serious complaints. Amanda was even able to clear out the stack of folders and memos that usually cluttered her desk.

"I can actually see the top of it," she boasted to Connie as they sat in a booth at Kovac's, where they had gone for a quick lunch. They didn't eat out together often because of their unpredictable schedules. Usually lunch was a quick meal in the hospital cafeteria whenever they could find time to slip away.

Although the two women shared an apartment, they spent relatively little time together. For the most part, they were occupied with their jobs, and on weekends they rarely saw each other since Connie often visited her family.

Connie sighed happily as she sampled the creamy broccoli soup and the crisp salad with Sophie's special dressing. "If I could learn to make soup like this, I'd cook dinner for us every night and let you do all the housework," she said.

"If you could make soup like this, there'd be a waiting list of hungry guys wanting to come to dinner," Amanda answered. "That's the trouble with our schedules. Neither one of us has time to really learn how to cook. The best I can do is a microwave chicken dish."

"I know. You're a really great counselor, Amanda," Connie said with a grin, "but you're a disaster in the kitchen. When you get beyond tuna sandwiches, you're lost."

Amanda ignored her roommate's teasing while she savored a spoonful of soup. "I'll learn when I get the time. Right now, I just give thanks for Sophie."

"Did someone call my name?" a hearty voice rang out. They looked up to see that the restaurant's owner had stopped at their table.

"Connie was just telling me I'd starve if I had to survive on my own cooking," Amanda said. "I don't know what we'd do without you, Sophie."

"Glad to hear it. When folks get to where they can cook better than I can, I'm in trouble."

Sophie Kovac was a good-natured woman with a ready smile and a genuine affection for people. She loved to see her customers enjoy the food she served. "Things must be slow at the hospital. I've had a heavy trade from over there this week," she commented.

"For some odd reason, everything has been running very smoothly," Connie said. "The lull won't last long, of course."

"By the way, that good-looking doctor you brought in here last week has been back twice. He likes my cooking," Sophie said to Amanda. "And I must say, he can use some good food. These young bachelors never get a decent meal."

"How do you know he's a bachelor?" Amanda asked.

"Because he wouldn't be here if he weren't. A handsome fellow like him would be at home eating his wife's cooking. You can always tell the bachelors, anyhow. They look hungry," Sophie said with a chuckle. "And speaking of being hungry, I've got your favorite lemon meringue pie today. Just thought you'd like to know."

Connie and Amanda exchanged glances. "Shall we?" Amanda asked hopefully.

"Of course. If we take the stairs instead of the elevator a few times, we can make up for the calories. And meringue has no cholesterol,'' Connie pointed out.

"Two lemon meringue pies it is, then,'' Sophie said. As she turned away, she called back over her shoulder to Amanda, "By the way, your good-looking doctor asked about you both times he came in.''

Connie's eyes narrowed as she looked at Amanda. "What doctor? Who were you with?''

"I brought Ross McKinnon in one evening so that we could talk about one of his cases,'' Amanda said, a flush starting up her cheeks.

"Dr. McKinnon?'' Connie's interest sharpened. "What's he like? Is he as abrupt off-duty as he is at the hospital?''

"He really isn't abrupt when you get to know him. It's just that he's unbelievably busy,'' Amanda explained. "He works really long hours.''

"I take it that you've had a change of heart about him since you two had your run-in.''

"Just a better understanding. I have more appreciation of the demands on him, and he seems willing to try to see Social Service's point of view. It's just that he's so pressed for time and really needs all the help he can get. That's why I brought him to Kovac's. He needs a place close to the hospital where he can get some decent food.''

"You seem to have become quite a fan of

Ross's,'' Connie observed, giving her a meaningful glance.

''If admiring him for being a fine, caring doctor makes me a fan, then I definitely am one,'' Amanda admitted. Then she quickly shifted the conversation to other topics.

Later, as Amanda set out on her afternoon appointments, she found herself thinking about Ross. It was reassuring to know that he had been back to Kovac's. At least he would get a few nutritious meals. He was meticulous about his patients, but he seemed to be terribly neglectful of himself. She decided he needed looking after.

Amanda saw nothing of Ross for the rest of the week. Nor did he appear at the Friday-afternoon meeting of Tony's rehab team. Instead, Dr. Foster relayed his report to the assembled members of the team.

''Dr. McKinnon is satisfied with Tony's recovery from surgery and plans to release him from the hospital early next week. He's prescribing continuing physical therapy for him on an outpatient basis and is leaving it up to us to work out an effective program. I'd like to hear your recommendations,'' he concluded.

One by one, the reports were made by the therapists and nursing representatives. All of them concurred. While he participated dutifully in the programs prescribed for him, Tony had a total lack of enthusiasm.

"His hand dexterity has come along well," Abby Simms, the occupational therapist, reported. "But he still hasn't regained the arm strength he had before his injury. It would help if he were more determined about his recovery."

"It's the same with his physical therapy," Connie reported. "He goes through the motions with his exercises, but he isn't really exerting much effort. I think he has the idea that his houseman, Sam, who is a sort of trainer to him, can work with him better at home, but the ordinary type of workout won't do for him. I'm afraid if Tony persists in going his own stubborn way, he could be in trouble."

"I agree," Ann Smythe said. "Although he's more cooperative with the staff, it's only because he's no longer as restricted in his activity. He follows the orders he feels like going along with and ignores those he doesn't like. For example, we nurses have to watch him constantly to see that he wears his neck brace."

"I find the same disturbing attitude," the vocational therapist, Rob Miller, said. "We've tried to make him understand that he's going to have to make some changes, but he belittles all our suggestions and refuses to consider any alternatives. If Tony can't change his thinking, he could eventually end up with an even worse injury than this one.''

Dr. Foster nodded regretfully. ''I'm sorry to say that both Dr. McKinnon and I have come to the same conclusion. We can give Tony our informed opinions; unfortunately we can't make him follow our advice.''

There was disappointment among the team members, who always considered it a failure when a patient didn't recover fully. Tony's case was particularly frustrating for them because of his wasted potential.

''We'll go ahead with Tony as if we expect his full cooperation,'' Dr. Foster concluded. ''I'll combine your recommendations into a program that I'll present to him when he leaves the hospital. Dr. McKinnon and I will both emphasize its importance, and I'd like Amanda to try once more to get him to see his situation realistically. Beyond that, there's nothing more we can do. Tony will have to make the decision to let us help him.''

Amanda left the meeting discouraged. She wondered what she was going to say to Tony. *How do you convince a person he needs help when he is determined not to be convinced?* she wondered.

By Monday, Amanda had thought of no new way to approach Tony. Although he was being released the following day, she wasn't confident that she could get through to him.

Late in the afternoon, as she sat at her desk pondering the problem, her thoughts were interrupted by a telephone call. A familiar voice came over the line. "Amanda, I need your help."

"Ross?" she said, recognizing the strong, vibrant tones.

"Yes. I've got a tough job for you. If you can meet me in the staff lounge in NICU right now, I'd like to tell you about it."

All thoughts of Tony fled from her mind as she set out for the Neurological Intensive Care Unit. The patients in the unit were always in serious condition. If Ross was asking for help with one of them, it could mean that someone was in real trouble.

She found him waiting for her in the lounge, sipping a cup of the strong, rancid coffee that usually simmered in the coffeepots by late afternoon. She shook her head as she entered the room, instinctively blurting out her disapproval. "You shouldn't be drinking that stuff. It's like battery acid. Juice is much better for you. What kind do you like best?" Marching to the cabinet at the side of the room, she reached inside to select one of the cans of juice that were stored there.

He grinned. "Hey, *I'm* not the patient."

"You will be if you don't do something about your diet," she said sternly.

"I surrender. Make it some kind of citrus punch. That ought to mix well with battery acid."

She filled a paper cup with ice and poured in the juice. He took a sip and nodded in approval. "Not bad. I can handle this." His expression sobered then. "Get yourself a cup of juice too while I tell you about my patient. This kid is in big trouble, and I thought maybe there was something you could do to help him."

Amanda listened with growing concern as Ross outlined his patient's situation. Billy Ray Johnson, aged twenty-two, had been riding his motorcycle to work that morning. Traveling on one of the more heavily traveled local freeways, he had been riding behind an eighteen-wheel truck. When the truck's driver slammed on the air brakes to avoid a stalled car, Billy Ray's bike had gone into a skid as he tried to stop suddenly. The skid had slammed him into the truck, and he had suffered a serious head injury. He was alive but in a coma, and his chances for survival were questionable. The next hours would be critical ones.

Billy Ray's young wife, with their year-old son, had been at the hospital all day, but she was too distraught to supply more than minimal information. According to her, the little family had no hospitalization insurance and an uncertain income.

Twenty-year-old Kitty Johnson was facing a devastating crisis with few if any resources to help her meet it.

"She's really in trouble," Ross concluded. "When I tried to talk to Kitty, I could see that she was terrified. She's beside herself with worry over Billy Ray and doesn't seem to understand the medical facts we're dealing with. The nurses in the waiting room finally figured out that neither she nor the baby had eaten all day and finally scared up a tray of food for them. She didn't want to take it because she said she couldn't pay for it. They finally convinced her it wouldn't cost anything, but they said she saved most of the food for the baby."

"She probably hasn't got any money," Amanda suggested.

"I would guess not," he agreed. "Anyhow, I suggested that we call you in. I know you'll pull all the strings you can to help her. Maybe you can talk to her and help her understand what we're trying to do for Billy Ray."

Amanda didn't need to talk to Kitty to know what a difficult spot she was in. Even if her husband survived his accident, there was a long road ahead for the couple. A whole battery of social services was needed to help them through this crisis.

"You can be sure I'll do everything I can for her," Amanda promised.

"I'll introduce you. She's so frightened right

now that she won't talk to anybody. She seems to accept my authority, though, and maybe I can convince her you're trying to help—although I'm not much good at that sort of thing.'' Ross offered Amanda a faint, apologetic smile. ''This one is a real bummer. I'm sorry I'm dumping it on you. I've got Billy Ray and another critical patient in there to see to.'' He gestured toward the curtained cubicles in the intensive-care section.

''I can take it from here. You do your job, and I'll do mine,'' Amanda reassured him.

''Thanks. Let me know how you do.'' He rose from his seat on the lumpy vinyl sofa and walked with her through the swinging doors of the treatment area to the visitors' lounge outside.

The NICU waiting room was, as always, filled with worried people. Even so, Amanda picked Kitty Johnson from among them at once. She sat huddled in a chair in one corner of the room, a forlorn-looking young woman holding a fidgety baby. Ross made the introductions and left.

Kitty was barely more than a teenager. She was small and slender with long brown hair and a child's round face and innocent eyes. In a happier time, she would likely have been exceptionally pretty. Under the present circumstances, she was terrified beyond any comprehension of the tragedy that had befallen her.

Amanda sat down beside her and spoke softly.

"Dr. McKinnon is doing everything he can for your husband, and I've come to see how I can help you. But first I have to get some information."

Kitty didn't reply, only stared at Amanda with wide, expressionless eyes.

"Did anyone come to the hospital with you?"

She shook her head.

"How did you find out about your husband's accident?"

"The hospital called me. They found our number in Billy Ray's wallet."

"How did you get here?"

"A deliveryman at the motel brought us."

"You're staying at a motel?"

"We've got a room there. I work as a maid for our rent."

Amanda moved to a new line of questioning. "Do you have any relatives you want to call?"

"We don't have any family here."

"We can call them in another city if necessary."

Kitty shook her head miserably. "They wouldn't come. They're mad at Billy Ray and me. They didn't want us to get married because they thought we were too young, so we ran away from home and did it anyway. They don't want anything to do with us now."

Amanda didn't follow up on the subject. There would be time later on to explore what was obviously a troubled family relationship. Right now, Kitty and the baby were the first priority.

She continued to question Kitty gently, taking time to win her confidence. Slowly, the young woman's resistance softened and Amanda was able to get a picture of the couple's situation.

From the time Billy Ray and Kitty Johnson defied their parents and got married, they had been in serious financial trouble. Ill-equipped to earn a living, Billy Ray had found work scarce. The arrival of their baby son made his situation all the more difficult. The little family had survived as best it could while he moved from job to job.

The Johnsons had come to the city only recently when Billy Ray had found a job as a dock loader for a moving company. Unfortunately, his job hadn't lasted, and he was able to get only temporary employment on a daily basis ever since. Running out of funds, they had been forced to sell their car, and Billy Ray had bought the motorcycle as a less-expensive means of transportation to work. They were barely managing to get by while he looked for a steady job.

Since the accident, Kitty had been living from moment to moment, waiting for news of her husband, too distraught to think about herself or the baby. Amanda was able to determine that she had no money and no supplies for the baby. She appeared to be in a daze, oblivious to their physical needs.

Having obtained the basic information she needed, Amanda set to work. Calling on the resources of the Social Services Department and hospital auxiliary services, she arranged for diapers and milk for the baby and food for the two of them. She borrowed an infant car bed from the hospital nursery that could serve as a makeshift crib for the baby. With these temporary provisions, the mother and child could manage for the next critical hours while Billy Ray's life hung by a thread. Tomorrow, Amanda would begin the complicated task of tapping into the network of social programs designed to help unfortunate people like the Johnsons.

Observing the frightened young mother, huddled desolately in the chair, and the now-exhausted baby who slept in her arms, Amanda felt a wrench of pity. The Johnsons were going to need all the help she could give.

Chapter Five

Amanda set to work early the following morning, contacting the various social-service agencies from whom she would solicit help for the Johnson family. By midmorning, she had obtained temporary support to see Kitty through the next difficult days. Although Billy Ray's job had been only temporary, his employer was understanding and cooperative. He agreed to send Billy Ray's accumulated wages, such as they were, to Kitty. The owner of the motel where the Johnsons lived was equally cooperative, consenting to hold their room and Kitty's job through the emergency. A conference with a representative from the hospital insurance office set in motion a search for help with

Billy Ray's hospital expenses. For the time being, at least, the Johnsons could get along.

Amanda's work had, of course, produced a stack of forms requiring Ross's signature. She decided to deliver them to his office with an explanatory note, as they had agreed.

Laurie Collins promised to help process the papers. "We've started a new system that ought to work much better in handling this sort of thing. We'll be in closer touch with Dr. McKinnon throughout the day. We can do a better job for him and for everyone else concerned." She offered Amanda a grateful smile. "I don't know what you told him, but he seems to have a much better understanding of the demands on other departments in the hospital."

"I think maybe I have a better understanding of the demands on him," Amanda said. "You have to follow him around for a day to find out how really busy he is."

"If you're lucky enough to be able to find him long enough to follow him," Laurie said with an exasperated shrug. "I've never worked for a doctor who could get from one place to another as fast as he does. Keeping up with him is like chasing a shadow. Just when you think you've got hold of him, he's gone."

Amanda had to laugh at the description. "I'm sure it's not an easy job."

"But a very rewarding one. He's really a nice guy when he gets time." Laurie's attention moved to a stack of memos on her desk. "By the way, he called in a while ago and left a message for you. He said he's going to be in and out of NICU for the next few hours and that if you wanted to see him, the desk would page him."

"Did he say how Billy Ray Johnson was doing?"

"He said there was no change. I don't know if that's good or bad."

Amanda looked at her watch. "I had planned to go by the NICU lounge and talk to Kitty Johnson before lunch. Maybe I'll try to check with Ross while I'm there."

"He seemed to expect you would," Laurie said. Her eyes were curious as she watched Amanda set out for NICU.

Kitty was still in the lounge where she had waited yesterday. Today, however, she sat on a sofa beside Mrs. Stone, the grandmother of another patient in NICU, who was quietly playing with the baby.

"I see he's found a friend," Amanda said as she approached.

"Beejee's a love," Mrs. Stone said. "Such a sweet, patient little fellow. Doesn't cry at all."

Beejee seemed to be well-cared-for and well-nourished. Even in her distracted state, Kitty was giving him lots of affection. Her hand rested tenderly on his shoulder as he lay beside her on the sofa, kicking and gurgling contentedly with his attention fixed on Mrs. Stone, who talked softly to him.

"I've got some encouraging news for you," Amanda said as she pulled up a chair and sat down beside Kitty. "I've talked to your employer at the hotel, and he says you're not to worry about your job or your room. He said to tell you your friends at the motel are concerned about Billy Ray and want to help however they can. They'll be glad to drive you back and forth to the hospital."

A worried frown crossed Kitty's face. "I don't want to leave Billy Ray."

"I understand how you feel, but at some point you and Beejee have to go home and get some rest."

"But Billy Ray might wake up and I wouldn't be here."

Amanda didn't want to say that as serious as Billy Ray's head injury was, he wasn't likely to recognize anyone for a while. "Right now, there really isn't anything you can do for him," she pointed out instead. "It's better if you go home and change clothes and gather some strength for the time when he'll need you."

"That's good advice, dear," Mrs. Stone spoke up. "This could go on for a while, you know. My grandson has been here for over a week. In the meantime, his parents have to go to work and take

care of their other children. We take turns coming
to the hospital now.''

Mrs. Stone seemed to have a settling effect on
Kitty. She had apparently struck up a friendship
with the young mother and baby. Amanda took
advantage of the chance to talk to Kitty about more
immediate and practical matters. ''I can try to get
you some help with Beejee if you'd like me to,''
she suggested. ''There is child care available in the
hospital. You could leave Beejee there while you're
waiting with Billy Ray.''

''You ought to think about it,'' Mrs. Stone
agreed. ''This little fellow could use a nice crib to
sleep in.''

''But Billy Ray might wake up and want to see
him,'' Kitty said doubtfully. ''He's crazy about
Beejee.''

''Then it would ease him to know that his son
is being looked after properly,'' Mrs. Stone pointed
out. ''The best thing you can do for your husband
right now is take care of your baby and yourself.''

''While you think about it, I'll go and see if I
can get some information about your husband,''
Amanda volunteered.

Amanda left word with the nurse at the NICU
desk to page Ross and went to the staff lounge to
wait for him. He appeared a short time later, seeming pleased to see her. She gave him a quick report
on the Johnson family.

He nodded, satisfied. "If Billy Ray comes around, it'll help him to know that his wife and son are taken care of. His wife has to understand, though, that it will be a while before we even know what we're dealing with. Billy Ray is stable now, but that's about all. He hasn't regained consciousness, and he may not recognize her if he does."

"Do you have any idea when he might regain consciousness?" Amanda asked.

Ross shook his head. "With a head injury like this, there's nothing to do but wait. It all depends on how much damage there has been to the brain. Right now, this could go either way."

"I hate the thought of explaining that to Kitty, but I suppose she has to know," Amanda said regretfully.

"Then don't try to explain it to her. Let the nurses handle it. It's their job, and they know how to do it," he said. He smiled at her. "Some wise person was telling me only yesterday, I think, that I should do my job and let her do hers. I thought it was good advice."

"I see what you mean," she said, chastened. "I guess it's always easier to give advice than it is to take it."

He chuckled. "Always. But thanks for doing your job so well. I knew you'd come through for Kitty, and I'll let you know how things go with Billy Ray."

"I'd appreciate it, although I can keep informed through the nurses. I know how busy you are."

"Not that busy. I think I can manage to find time for you," he said. His lips curved into a smile that set Amanda's heart to pounding. At that moment, she decided that there was definitely nothing cold and distant about Ross McKinnon.

She took his advice to heart and gave Kitty only a brief report on Billy Ray, explaining that the nurse on duty at the NICU desk would keep her informed about his condition. She promised to check back with her later on in the day concerning Beejee's care and then moved on to the other duties that needed her attention.

One of those duties was a final visit to Tony, and it wasn't a task she looked forward to. She had little hope of convincing Tony to be realistic—or to do anything else, for that matter. She feared that Tony was going to do what he wanted, think what he wanted, and believe what he wanted in spite of anything anybody could say to him.

Amanda found Tony in bright spirits that afternoon. Dressed in workout togs and athletic shoes, he wore only a light collar as a neck brace. Seated in the armchair in his room with a briefcase in his lap, he was leafing through a stack of business papers.

"I see you're back at work," Amanda said. "I'm sure you're glad to be going home in the morning."

"Assuming that Dr. Doom doesn't come up with some other form of torture before he agrees to release me," he quipped. "I'm sure he'll want to get in a last lick."

Amanda bristled at Tony's sarcasm. If it wasn't for Ross's skill, this man might still be lying helpless in bed. "I'm sure Dr. McKinnon will be just as pleased to release you as you'll be to go home," she told Tony.

He held up an apologetic hand. "I get the message, and I'm truly penitent. You've all done your best to patch me up, and I know I've been a miserable, ungrateful patient. I've made a pledge to try to make it up to you—*after* I get out of here, of course."

"You can thank us best by making a successful recovery."

"The thanks I had in mind was a little more personal, but the recovery will definitely help things along." There was no mistaking the challenge in his words or the invitation in his smile. Amanda had to concede that Tony, with his dark, flashing eyes and even white teeth, was an extremely attractive man. He was also fully aware of his masculine appeal and was making the most of it. It was definitely time for him to get back to his own life.

She returned determinedly to the subject of her visit. "Your recovery is what I'd like to talk to you about. From now on, your progress is going to depend on yourself, and we'd like to think you're going to be realistic."

He raised an eyebrow. "There's that word again. They've been shoving it at me all day. I guess they're sending the angel of mercy for a last go at me." He closed his briefcase and assumed a dutiful position in his chair, reminding Amanda of a recalcitrant child who was resigned to a scolding. "Go ahead, gorgeous. Lay it on me."

Amanda wrestled with her exasperation. "I'm not going to preach to you, Tony. You're an intelligent man. You've been told by a team of medical experts what you can reasonably expect from your recovery and what you're going to have to do to accomplish it. Yet so far you've ignored their advice and resisted treatment."

"In other words, I'm a lousy patient," Tony said with a roguish grin.

"Sick people often aren't cooperative. We're used to dealing with them. The patient who frustrates us the most is the one who refuses to be sensible about himself. You're really very lucky, you know. You have the opportunity to return to a normal, productive life, provided you can accept a few restrictions on a few risky activities."

"What if I don't want a normal life?"

"At least you have a choice. Some people don't. They have to make the best of physical limitations they can do nothing about. It's quite possible, you know, to find your thrills and excitement without taking risks."

"Now there's an interesting thought," he said with another suggestive smile.

Amanda ignored his insinuation, but it was all she could do to control her impatience. It was clear that she was wasting her time with Tony. He refused to be serious about anything she said.

She turned toward the door and, in her most professional tone, ended the conversation. "As I said, you have a choice. In any case, we wish you well. Please let us know if you need any more help from us."

"Oh, you'll be hearing from me," he said with a grin. "That's a promise."

Amanda turned away with a feeling of defeat. She had accomplished nothing. He hadn't changed his attitude. Whatever drove him along his willful path of self-destruction was still as strong as before his accident.

At the end of the workday, Amanda paid a visit to NICU for a last check on Kitty. She was hoping Kitty had recovered from her shock well enough to make some practical decisions.

Kitty was seated in her customary spot. Beejee

was sleeping peacefully in his makeshift bed. As Amanda approached them, Kitty regarded her anxiously. "I was hoping you'd stop by. I have some questions for you," she said.

"That's why I'm here." Amanda gave her an encouraging smile. She noticed a large duffel bag on the floor beside Kitty. "I see you got some things together. Did you get out of the hospital today?"

Kitty shook her head. "Some friends from the motel brought us some clothes. They've really been nice to us."

"People always surprise you with their kindness at a time like this. They truly want to help," Amanda said.

"They've offered to drive me back and forth from the hospital, but I don't want to leave until Billy Ray is better. So they brought us some pillows and blankets, and we're going to stay here again tonight. Maybe by morning he'll be able to talk to us."

"Have you made any decision about Beejee? The waiting is bound to be hard on him."

"He's used to waiting around with me and doesn't bother anybody. Besides, I want him close to Billy Ray. He's named for his daddy, you know—Billy Ray, Jr. We couldn't decide whether to call him Billy or Ray, and we didn't want to call him Junior. Finally, his daddy started calling him

Beejee.'' Kitty interrupted her rambling monologue to look up at Amanda with anxious eyes. ''That's why I want him to be here with me. Billy Ray will want to see him as soon he wakes up, and that could happen anytime. The nurse told me the next twenty-four hours are critical.''

The news had an ominous sound to Amanda, but she remembered Ross's advice and made no comment. She settled for explaining to Kitty once again that she could call the Social Services offices for her anytime. After chatting with the young woman for a few more minutes, she left her to her vigil. At the moment, there was nothing more she could do for the Johnson family.

As Amanda left the waiting room and started down the corridor to the elevator, she couldn't help comparing Billy Ray to Tony. With a severe head injury like Billy Ray's, there could be brain damage. If he lived through the next twenty-four hours, there was no predicting what physical impairment he might face. On the other hand, Tony had not only survived a serious spinal injury but had recovered from it almost fully. Yet he seemed to have no appreciation of his good fortune.

Amanda couldn't help feeling impatient with Tony, who had so much to be thankful for. She had to remind herself that it was not her place to judge him. Hard as it was at times, she needed to remember that, in a different way, Tony was a sick man too.

As she stood deep in thought waiting for an elevator to stop at the floor, she felt a light touch on her shoulder. "You're very solemn this evening," a familiar voice said. "You look as though you're carrying the weight of the world on your shoulders."

She looked up to see Ross standing beside her. "I guess I'm a little tired. It's been a long and rather discouraging day. Incidentally, I just left Kitty. She gave me a report on Billy Ray that didn't sound very good."

"He's developing some problems that we're watching closely. We have our work cut out for us." He looked at her curiously. "Speaking of work, I take it that yours is giving you problems again too."

"Only the usual."

"I know what you mean. Maybe it would help us both to get away from problems for a while. I want to stay close to the hospital, but I could really stand a breather. If you haven't any other plans, maybe we could get something to eat at Kovac's? I could use the company if you've got the time." His lips curved in an inviting smile.

Amanda's heart flipflopped. Suddenly, she had all the time in the world. "I'd love to."

"Then why don't I meet you at Kovac's in an

hour or so? First one there gets a table. Maybe if we go separately by the back way, we can sneak out of the hospital without running into someone who has something for one of us to do,'' he said conspiratorially.

''We can try,'' Amanda said.

Her discouragement had already vanished by the time she stepped on the elevator. The evening suddenly seemed exciting, and Kovac's seemed the most glamorous place. She couldn't think of anything she'd rather do than have dinner with Ross.

Well, almost anything, she corrected herself.

Chapter Six

The dinner hour at Kovac's was quiet and relaxed, free of the bustle of the noon diners who had to hurry to meet afternoon schedules. With the onset of twilight, Sophie brought out candles in colored glass lamps, lending a festive touch to the dining room.

Amanda arrived before Ross and ordered a glass of mineral water to sip on while she waited for him. He arrived a short time later, looking a bit harried. "I hope you haven't been waiting long. I got hung up."

"I've been here only a little while," she assured him. "It's nice to sit here peacefully."

"Then we'll try to keep it that way. No talk

about the hospital or patients tonight,'' he said, sliding into the chair beside her.

She smiled. ''Fine with me.''

He returned her smile. ''To be honest, what I really had in mind was simply enjoying some good company.''

In this relaxed, informal setting, Ross gave quite a different impression. In his sport jacket and open-collared shirt, he seemed much younger and light-hearted than the preoccupied doctor she was accustomed to seeing. His eyes held a glint of humor; his speech was softer and less clipped. It occurred to Amanda what a very attractive, appealing man he was, and she suddenly felt shy and wary. It wouldn't do to harbor such thoughts about a man like him. It would not only be totally unprofessional but also very foolish. Handsome, unattached doctors like Ross had their pick of glamorous women.

The observation led to another, more pertinent question. What made her think he was, in fact, unattached? For all she knew, he could be romantically involved with someone—maybe even engaged. It was a disconcerting possibility that she guiltily dismissed, along with her unsuitable thoughts about his personal life.

Whatever his status, Ross turned out to be a congenial dinner companion. After they had placed their orders, he led the conversation away from the concerns of the hospital, as he had promised. They talked of inconsequential subjects until he suddenly stopped in midsentence. "Amanda, I don't want to spend the next hour probing politely for information about you. I'd hate to get right to the point of finding out what I want to know and get called back to the hospital before I got my answer." He leaned forward to study her intently. "Tell me, are you married?"

"Of course not," she said, startled. "I wouldn't be here if I were."

He seemed pleased. "That's good to know. I'm not married, either, and I also wouldn't be here if I were." His expression became curious then. "Is there a steady boyfriend in the picture?"

She shook her head. "No, although I'm not sure that's to my credit."

"I know what you mean. I keep thinking that, at my age, I ought to have found somebody special, but I've never had time for much of a social life. I'm surprised, though, that a pretty woman like you wasn't snapped up long ago by some lucky guy."

"Hardly. I've been too busy studying and training and working. I haven't had time for personal relationships."

"Neither have I." He smiled at her ingenuously. "Anyhow, I just thought I'd set the record straight. I didn't want to move in on some other guy's territory."

Amanda was too surprised to answer. Fortunately, their food arrived at the table, interrupting the conversation. After they were served, Ross moved on to another subject. During the course of the meal, however, they learned a great deal about each other. Ross revealed that he was from a small town in Vermont, where his parents still lived. He had a younger sister who was married and the mother of two little boys. He had received his medical training in Boston and then had come to City Medical Center to enter practice with two older neurosurgeons.

In turn, Amanda revealed that she had one brother, who lived in California, and parents who still occupied the family home in Virginia where she had grown up. With its members living such distances apart, it was a rare treat for the Summerses to be together. Lacking any family close by, she welcomed the opportunity to share an apartment with Connie. Although Connie still spent most weekends with her family, the arrangement had worked very well. The two friends went their separate ways without crowding each other, but each was ready to supply a sympathetic ear when the need arose.

''It's surprising, in a way, that we get along as well as we do,'' Amanda confided. ''Coming from a large, noisy family, Connie likes things quiet. I, on the other hand, like to come home from work and listen to music. My mother teaches piano, and there was always music in the background at our house. To me, a house is lonely without it. When Connie is at home, I use headphones, but on the weekends I can turn up the stereo and have music all around me.''

He nodded enthusiastically. "I'm with you. I like to tune everything out when I come in at night. I rented this top-floor apartment that has a balcony and a big living-room window that looks out over the city skyline. In decent weather, I can go outside and kick back for a while, looking at the lights and listening to music."

"We don't have much of a balcony, but we can see the city lights. I like to look out at them and listen to classical music," Amanda confided. "That's what I heard when I was growing up, and it's soothing to me."

"No rap, rock, or rhythm and blues?"

"I like those at the right time, but it makes me feel sort of ragged after a trying day. A big, full symphony sweeps all the stress away."

He looked at her curiously. "You're full of surprises, Mandy. By the way, do you mind me calling you by that name? Somehow it seems to suit you."

"My brother used to call me that, but nobody else ever did."

"I guess it's the color of your hair. Or maybe. . . ." He studied her critically. "Maybe it's the three freckles you've got on the tip of your nose.''

Amanda's hand flew to her face to cover the offending marks. ''I didn't know they were so noticeable. Maybe I need more makeup.''

''No way. I like your freckles. They're distinctive. They keep you from looking too serious and professional.''

They spent the rest of the meal in lighthearted banter, lingering over dessert and coffee. Ross seemed reluctant to end the occasion, and they strolled slowly back to the hospital. He walked Amanda to her car and stopped with her beside it, seeming to want to prolong the evening.

After a moment's silence, he asked suddenly, ''Have you ever done any fishing?''

''Not lately. But I used to go fishing with my dad when I was a little girl.''

''I keep a boat at a lake not too far from the city so that I can slip away when I get the chance. Fishing does for me what your classical music does for you.'' He hesitated, then asked, ''Would you go fishing with me sometime?''

Amanda didn't need to consider her answer. ''I'd love to,'' she said.

''Then I'll call you when I have a free weekend.'' He waited until she was settled in her car, then, placing a hand on her shoulder, he said, ''Thanks for the evening, Mandy. You're fun to be around.''

He waited until she had driven away before he started back toward the hospital. As she turned out of the parking lot, she caught sight of his tall figure silhouetted against the lights of the emergency entrance. She smiled contentedly. She was finding Ross fun to be around too.

The next morning brought encouraging news. Billy Ray Johnson had recovered consciousness during the night. The extent of his recovery was still uncertain, but at least he had recognized Kitty and was able to speak to her. Greatly relieved, Kitty was able to think practically about their problems. She accepted Amanda's offer to arrange day care for Beejee and began to make plans for coping with Billy Ray's stay in the hospital.

The rest of the week passed smoothly. Amanda's work was routine. There were no thorny problems to solve, no difficult patients to contend with. She referred several patients to support groups for their particular illnesses, processed a request for temporary home care for an elderly patient through the visiting-nurse program, and arranged a transfer to a convalescent center for a patient who needed special care.

She was also assigned to a new rehab team. Greg Carter, a college student, had suffered a spinal injury in a diving accident, requiring him to undergo rehabilitative therapy to regain the use of his legs.

Greg refused to be daunted by his injury and, unlike Tony, was working hard to make a full recovery. An inspiration to other patients and an encouragement to the therapists, he had quickly become a favorite in the rehab department.

Connie had been assigned as Greg's physical therapist and was dedicated to his recovery. "Greg is the kind of patient who reminds you why you went into this field in the first place," she said. "He's going to walk out of this hospital unaided if there's any way in the world I can help him do it."

Watching Connie work with Greg one afternoon while she was passing through the physical therapy area, Amanda had no doubt that the two of them would eventually achieve their goal. He had progressed to full-length braces and, cumbersome though they were, could stand alone between the parallel walking bars. Amanda lingered for a moment to watch with admiration while he practiced walking.

She felt a hand fall lightly on her shoulder and turned to see Tony smiling down at her. "Hi, gorgeous," he said with a smile. "Have you missed me as much as I've missed you?"

Tony seemed to have made an impressive recovery. He looked trim and fit, wearing an expensive camel's-hair sport coat, well-fitting slacks, and a white knit shirt that emphasized his athletic physique. His black hair swept across his brow attractively, and his dark eyes sparkled with high spirits. Although he still wore a neck brace, he seemed to have adjusted to it.

"You're looking very well," she said. "I take it that you're feeling better."

"Much better. In fact, I'm almost back in racing form except for this." He tapped a manicured forefinger to the collar that encircled his neck.

Amanda couldn't suppress a rush of exasperation at his incredibly poor judgment. "I suppose we all have our priorities."

His lips curved into a roguish smile. "Actually, I don't plan to race again. I'm sponsoring a young driver who has oil in his blood and wants to make a run of it."

How typical it was of Tony to consider it a heroic gesture to enable somebody else to do himself in, Amanda thought ironically. "As I said, our priorities seem to differ."

He shrugged. "To each his own. For myself, I'm finding that the polo circuit has new appeal these days. I've had my string of ponies brought up from Florida and I'm getting them ready to play. I'm not riding, of course," he added hastily, "at least not until Dr. Doom has removed this vise from my neck."

The total arrogance of this man! Amanda

thought scornfully. No amount of surgeon's skill could save him from his own stupidity.

Although she didn't reply to his comment, he seemed to read her thoughts. It was a relief to see Connie and Greg coming toward them. Having finished his daily therapy, Greg was back in his wheelchair, propelling himself expertly while Connie tried to keep pace with him. He spun to a perfect stop next to Amanda.

"How's that for technique?" he asked with a flourishing gesture toward his wheelchair. "If I'd been this good a diver, I might be walking instead of riding."

"This is Greg Carter. He's recovering from a diving accident," Amanda explained to Tony.

"And doing very well," Connie said as she joined them. She nodded to Tony. "This is Tony Lawrence, Greg. He was one of our patients here in rehab."

Greg's eyes brightened with recognition. "You're the race-car driver, aren't you? I saw you on TV. That was some crash. You're lucky to have come out of it in such good shape."

"You could say that." Tony cast an amused glance at Connie. "In any case, it's good to be back in action. I expect you're anxious to get back to diving."

Greg shook his head vigorously. "I won't be

doing any more diving. I'll have to settle for a nice, easy swim.''

"That's too bad. It's hard to give up something you do so well.''

"I'll miss it, sure. I was in college on an athletic scholarship. But right now I'll just settle for getting back on my feet and in school.''

"First things first,'' Tony agreed. "Watching you, I'd say that you're making a fine recovery.''

"I'm getting there. I'll be satisfied if I do as well as you've done,'' Greg said. With a jaunty wave, he set off in his wheelchair to join the attendant who was waiting for him.

Tony watched thoughtfully as Greg wheeled himself down the corridor. He seemed a bit subdued when he turned back to Connie. "Don't say it.''

"I didn't make a sound,'' she protested.

"Then don't think it.'' He took off his jacket and gestured toward the treatment area. "Shall we get on with my checkup?''

"After you,'' Connie said with a grin.

Tony turned to Amanda. "Sorry to interrupt our conversation. It was just getting interesting. But I'll be back in touch with you *very* soon.'' He turned to follow Connie to an exercise table.

Amanda couldn't help feeling amused as she left Tony and Connie to their work. She had the feeling that he was chastened by his conversation with

Greg. Could it be that their imperious patient was finally experiencing a little humility?

Over the next few days, Amanda noticed that someone else had also become suddenly less imperious. The normally elusive Dr. McKinnon was displaying a singular availability. He called her office several times to offer or ask for information concerning a patient. To her surprise, he unexpectedly—and, it could be said, unnecessarily—attended a meeting of a rehab team of which she was a member, even though the team had only a small role in the treatment of one of his patients. On her visits to the neurological and surgical floors, his rangy figure seemed to materialize with astonishing frequency. It became a regular occurrence to find him suddenly strolling along beside her, talking companionably.

One afternoon, Amanda had just left a patient and was setting off toward the elevators when she heard his now-familiar voice call out her name. "Wait up," he said as he fell in beside her. "I need to ask you something."

She stopped walking and turned to face him. "What is it?" she asked with a smile.

He grinned. "Can we go someplace where we can talk?"

"Sure."

He looked furtively up and down the hall and

then took her by the hand and pulled her along
behind him as he ducked inside a nearby door.
"This ought to do. Nobody can see us in here."

"Are we hiding from somebody?"

"From everybody. If we stand out there in the
hall talking, somebody will find something for one
of us to do."

As he closed the door behind him, Amanda
looked around her in surprise. "Ross, this is a linen
closet."

"I know."

Recalling the stories of amorous encounters in
the proverbial hospital linen closet, Amanda cast a
suspicious glance at him. "I'll just bet you do."

He shrugged. "Actually, I haven't hidden out in
the linen closet since I was a first-year resident, but
knowledge once acquired comes back when
needed. You have to agree that privacy is hard to
come by at a hospital."

Amanda's heart began to beat a little faster as
she stood close to Ross in the confined space. She
was beginning to have some interesting thoughts
about how they might take advantage of their privacy. Shaking off the impulse, she turned to look
up at him primly. "What did you want to talk
about?"

He hesitated for a moment, his attention diverted
as he gazed down at her face. "It's those freckles,"
he mumbled distractedly. "Three of them, abso-

lutely perfectly aligned. The effect is amazing.''
Then he shook off the thought, drawing his attention away from the tip of her nose. "Actually, I wanted to talk to you about fishing."

Amanda's hopes plummeted. "Why do we need to go into a linen closet to talk about fishing?"

"So we won't be interrupted. There always seems to be a bunch of people around us."

She immediately thought of a way he could remedy the situation, but didn't suggest it. It was up to him to make the first move if he wanted to go out on a date with her.

He seemed to be thinking along the same lines. "I was thinking maybe we could get away from the hospital for a while. Did you mean it when you said you'd like to go fishing with me?"

"Of course I did."

"I'm due a Saturday off pretty soon. How about then?"

While it wasn't quite the romantic sort of outing Amanda might have dreamed of, any kind of invitation from Ross was better than none. "I think it would be fun," she said.

"Then I'll get in touch with you as soon as I'm sure which Saturday I'll be free. As the junior doctor in our practice, I have to cover most of the weekends, so I can't go very far from the hospital most of the time."

Amanda could think of a lot of things they could

be doing in the meantime, but she didn't mention them. It was enough that Ross was taking her out at all. ''Whenever,'' she said.

He nodded, seeming pleased. She made a move toward the door, thinking their conversation was finished. But he remained planted in her path, and she saw that his interest had strayed once again to her face. His attention was fixed—on her nose, perhaps. Or was it her lips?

Standing so close to him, she found that her own attention had been diverted. Somehow her glance had settled upon the intriguing curve of his lower lip. Their faces were only inches apart, and an invisible magnet seemed to be drawing them closer together.

''There's something I've been wanting to do,'' Ross said, mesmerized. He bent his head forward, and her lips melted into his in an irresistible kiss.

Amanda's senses were reeling, and she wanted it to go on and on. She made no effort to pull away until she became dimly aware that somebody had opened the door.

Stepping back quickly, she saw that Rose O'Bannon, one of the surgical nurses, stood in the doorway. Rose seemed to find nothing unusual in the scene, however, because her face was expressionless as she said, ''I'm sorry to interrupt, Dr. McKinnon, but they're almost ready for you in surgery.''

Ross regarded the nurse with unruffled detachment. "I'll be right there." If he was disconcerted by the ill-timed interruption, he gave no sign of it. Standing back, he gestured toward the door with a flourish. "After you, Ms. Summers," he said as he escorted Amanda from the linen closet with professional dignity.

Amanda gave the nurse a polite nod as she passed her. Without looking back, she continued on her way to the elevators. But once the doors closed behind her, she leaned weak-kneed against the wall, shaken by the unbelievable thing that had happened to her. Never would she have dreamed that one quick kiss could have such an amazing effect.

She should have been embarrassed to be caught in the closet kissing one of the doctors. Instead, her pulses were still racing five minutes later when she reached her office and sank down at her desk. Totally disconcerted by her reaction, she could only admonish herself sternly. If this was the way a single, simple kiss from him was going to affect her, she would do well to stay out of linen closets with Ross McKinnon.

Chapter Seven

Amanda was still shaken by her encounter with Ross when she arrived at her office the following morning. She had been able to think of little besides the kiss they had shared in the linen closet. With some difficulty, she forced her attention to the demands of the day. It was time to stop wool-gathering and get to work.

Bleakly, she regarded the stack of paperwork that sat on her desk. Somehow the papers that passed through the department seemed to multiply by themselves. She had settled down to work her way through the endless forms when the telephone rang.

"Do you know what day this is?" a cheerful voice asked.

Amanda smiled, recognizing Ross's voice. Her

glance settled on her desk calendar. "It's Friday," she replied.

"Do you know what tomorrow is?"

"Unless there's been an overnight change in our calendars, tomorrow is Saturday."

"It's more than a simple Saturday. I've managed to get the day off. I have an entire thirty-six hours when I won't be on call. What do you say we go fishing?"

Amanda's spirits soared. "What time?"

"How about five o'clock? We could be on the lake by sunrise."

"Sunrise?" Amanda's voice quavered at the thought of the early hour.

"That's when the fish bite best."

"Then I guess that's when we need to be there," she said doubtfully.

Ross burst out laughing. "I wouldn't think of dragging you out at such an hour. I'll pick you up at ten o'clock, and we'll take it from there."

He took down the directions to her apartment and hung up, leaving her pleased and excited. She returned to her work with enthusiasm.

The following morning dawned clear and sunny, promising to be a beautiful day. Dressed in jeans and a pullover, her hair held back by a headband, Amanda was ready to leave for the lake well before ten o'clock. Remembering her days of fishing with her father, she had prepared a picnic lunch. If the fish should start biting and Ross was the devoted fisherman he had indicated, some food might come in handy.

She had packed a Styrofoam cooler with turkey and watercress sandwiches, bunches of grapes, high-energy granola bars, and a thermos of fruit punch. The cooler, along with a portable radio and a fishing rod, sat beside the front door of the apartment, ready and waiting.

Ross arrived promptly at ten, and seemed surprised by Amanda's preparations. He said nothing, however, until they got to his car and he ceremoniously placed the cooler and radio in the backseat beside a second cooler and radio. "It appears that we've come well prepared," he said.

Amanda laughed. "Maybe we should have checked with each other."

"I thought you might like to listen to music while we fished," he explained.

"And I thought you might want to listen to the Saturday-afternoon football games. That's what my dad and I always did."

"Maybe we can work out some kind of a compromise." He shook his head in disbelief as he placed the fishing rod on the seat beside two others. "You really did come to fish, didn't you?"

"Of course. That's what you said we were going to do."

"I know, but I thought your idea of fishing might be dangling a pole over the side of the boat for a little while."

"Absolutely not. If we're going to fish, then let's do it right."

"You're one of a kind," he said as he slid into the driver's seat. They set out for the lake in high spirits.

An hour later, they were unloading their gear at a small A-frame lodge composed of one large room featuring a wide, stone fireplace, a compact galley kitchen, and an upstairs loft. Outside the wide window that overlooked the lake was a covered patio and a path that led to a dock extending out into the water. Anchored at the dock was a jaunty blue-and-white boat.

In minutes, they had loaded and launched the boat. Ross handled the boat expertly, giving Amanda a quick tour of the lake before they settled in to fish. It was a glorious day, mellow with sunshine and rich with the colors of early fall. The wind against their cheeks and the sparkle of the water foaming in their wake provided an exhilarating release from the bustle of the city. It felt good to be alive, to be outdoors enjoying the beauty of nature.

When Ross found the fishing spot he was seeking and anchored in a shady inlet, Amanda sighed contentedly. "This is an absolutely heavenly place. I can't think of a better way to spend a Saturday afternoon.''

''It's the place to come when you want to relax,'' he agreed. While he baited their hooks with purple plastic worms, which he guaranteed to be the most effective bait, Amanda found a football game on the portable radio.

They fished silently, listening to the drone of the radio, deftly casting into the water and reeling in their lines, waiting for a fish to take the lure. Amanda got the first strike and proudly reeled in a nice-size white bass, which she efficiently removed from the line and threaded onto the stringer that dangled in the water beside the boat.

Ross watched her in amazement. ''This is unbelievable. You're an honest-to-goodness *fisherman!*''

''Fisherwoman,'' she corrected him.

''Fisherperson, maybe?''

''Whatever. I just like to fish.'' She pointed to Ross's line, bobbing in the water. ''Speaking of fish, I think you're getting a bite.''

He turned his attention to his own fishing rod and promptly reeled in a catch of his own. They settled down to a serious pursuit of fishing.

It was long after lunchtime when, following a lull, Ross remembered the Styrofoam coolers they had loaded into the boat. ''I don't know about you, but I could do with a sandwich. Which cooler shall I open?''

''I guess that depends on what you want to eat.''

''What did you bring?'' he asked cautiously.

''I brought turkey sandwiches and grapes and granola bars. Just what the doctor ordered—all low fat, low cholesterol,'' Amanda said proudly. ''What did you bring?''

''I went by the deli and got pastrami sandwiches, dill pickles, potato chips, and sodas.''

''Just the kind of high-fat, high-sodium diet you'd never prescribe for your patients,'' Amanda accused.

He shrugged. ''I don't have to prescribe diets. I just repair people and let other doctors keep them healthy.''

She shook her head disapprovingly. ''Who keeps you healthy?''

''Nobody. Doctors simply self-destruct.''

''Not this doctor,'' Amanda threatened. ''You're going to get a proper lunch.'' She took out a turkey sandwich and a bunch of grapes and laid them on a paper napkin. Then she opened a package of premoistened hand towels and gave one to Ross. ''You can use this to wash the fish off your hands.''

''I don't worry much about aseptic conditions when I'm fishing.''

Amanda eyed him insistently while she washed her hands, cleaning each finger carefully and waiting until he followed her example. Then she filled a paper cup with fruit juice and handed it to him along with a turkey sandwich.

Ross bit into the sandwich hungrily. "This is great," he pronounced, wolfing it down in a few bites. "Do you have any more of those in there?"

She handed him the last of the turkey sandwiches and refilled his cup with fruit punch. Selecting one of the pastrami sandwiches he had brought, she poured a mound of chips onto a paper napkin, popped the top of a can of soda, and set in with relish to enjoy her lunch.

When they finished eating, Ross leaned back, munching on the last granola bar. "These are good. Maybe I ought to keep some of them in my office."

"They're a very good supply of energy," Amanda informed him, biting a pickle.

"Is that the last pickle?" He leaned over to peer into the two Styrofoam coolers. Amanda's was empty. His contained a single pastrami sandwich, a pickle, and a partially empty package of chips. He laughed. "All we did was end up eating each other's lunch."

"At least we shared the grapes," Amanda pointed out.

"But you got all the fat and cholesterol."

"And enjoyed every last gram of it."

"But what about your diet?"

"Nobody cares what social workers eat. Most people think they're kind of a nuisance anyhow."

Ross shook his head. "I don't know about social workers in general, but you are definitely not a nuisance."

Deciding to let the subject rest on that happy note, Amanda packed up the remains of their lunch and stowed the coolers. When they had tired of fishing, they enjoyed a boat ride across the lake before they returned to the lodge.

Ross announced that he intended to grill the fish they had caught for their dinner, promising Amanda a gourmet treat. While he cleaned and boned the fish, she seasoned the fillets and set them to marinate. As they worked, they listened to football scores and compared their favorite teams.

It was late afternoon by the time they finished their preparations. As the sun dipped low in the sky, Ross suggested a final boat ride. A slight evening chill had fallen over the lake, and the water was ablaze with the vermilion reflection of the setting sun. Amanda pulled her windbreaker around her and leaned back in her seat, enjoying the rush of the wind against her face and relishing the spectacular ending of a perfect day. As she glanced at Ross, admiring his profile silhouetted in the deepening dusk, she knew that this glorious day with him would be a memory she would always cherish.

When Ross idled the boat into its slip at the dock,

they sat for a moment, listening to the lapping of the water and admiring the last magenta rays of the vanishing sun. "This is the most beautiful sight I think I've ever seen." Amanda sighed contentedly. "This truly has been a wonderful day."

He seemed pleased by her response. "I thought you'd like it. A boat ride at sunset is like the icing on a cake."

After they had unloaded their gear, they secured the boat and covered it, reluctant for the day to end. By the time they started back up the path to the lodge, purple twilight had fallen and the quiet of evening had settled over the lake.

Ross refused Amanda's help with dinner. While the grill heated, he served them tall glasses of flavored seltzer and positioned a lounge chair so that Amanda could enjoy the view of the lake while she kept him company. He set up one of the radios, finding a program of soft, romantic music. "Sorry I can't find any Beethoven or Bach, but maybe this will do," he said as he set the radio beside her.

"It's perfect." Amanda leaned back in her chair, listening to the soft music. Admiring the lights that now dotted the lake and the first stars that had appeared in the sky, she thought she had never been happier.

Ross produced a dinner of perfectly grilled fish accompanied by scalloped potatoes and a tangy salad of asparagus and artichoke hearts. With a final flourish, he served a dessert of pound cake topped with chilled strawberries.

"That was a fantastic meal," Amanda exclaimed when she had finished the last crumb of the cake.

"All it takes is a few cans from the pantry, some boxes from the freezer, and a little imagination," Ross said proudly. "I'm not too bad in the kitchen when I get around to it. I'd never have made it through eight years of residency if I hadn't learned to put some kind of meal together."

"I think I should take some lessons from you," she said, thinking of her own limited cooking skills. Who would have thought that the impatient Dr. McKinnon would turn out to be a gourmet cook? Watching Ross, she decided that he was a totally unpredictable man.

They sat for a while after dinner, watching the stars and listening to music. When it was time to return to town, they were both reluctant to leave. Amanda cast a last regretful glance at the lodge as they locked the door.

Ross dropped an arm around her shoulders as they walked slowly to the car. "You enjoyed the day, didn't you?"

"I can't think of a better way—or a better place—to spend a Saturday. Thank you for bringing me with you. Actually, I feel like I know you better. At the hospital, you're so professional. But here at

the lake you're different, not so . . ." She searched
for a word. "Not so intimidating."

He seemed surprised. "Am I intimidating at the
hospital?"

"Let's say you run a tight ship. But then, isn't
that the way it should be? There isn't a lot of time
there to waste on pleasantries."

"Well, it must be the company." Looking down
into her face, he wrapped a lock of her hair around
his finger as he said softly, "When I'm around
you, I turn into a pussycat."

Amanda's breath caught in her throat. She had
a sudden longing to reach up and touch his cheek.
Confused by her sudden emotions, she could find
nothing to say. Ross had little to say, either, during
the drive back to town, but there was a comfortable
feeling between them. Something had changed in
their relationship. There was a closeness between
them that hadn't existed before, a contentment, an
understanding that didn't need expression.

When they turned off the main boulevard to reach
the street where Amanda lived, they passed the
hospital. Ross looked at the lit windows and said
with a trace of reluctance, "It's still there—and so
is Billy Ray Johnson. Even though I'm supposed
to be taking a weekend off, I can't help being
concerned about him. He wasn't doing very well
last night." He glanced questioningly at Amanda.
"Would you mind if I stopped at your apartment

and called in to check on him? If he's doing okay, I can go home and enjoy my Sunday with a clear conscience.''

"I'll do better than supply a telephone. I'll give you a cup of coffee, if you'd like," she said, not nearly ready for the evening to end.

At the apartment, after they had unloaded her fishing gear, Amanda put on coffee to brew while Ross made his call to the hospital. When she returned, his face was concerned. "Billy Ray's got problems. He isn't responding to his medication as he should, and I think I should stop by and check him over. Even though I'm off duty, I'd want to be called if things go bad for him.''

"It's serious, isn't it?" Amanda said, thinking of Kitty.

"He may not make it," Ross said. "We knew this could go one way or another. Right now it isn't looking very good.''

"I'm so sorry," Amanda said. "I've become interested in the Johnsons. They seem to be such happy kids in spite of all their problems. I was hoping he would make a turn for the better.''

"I thought maybe he had. He seemed to be responding to his medication, but now . . ." Ross shook his head doubtfully. "We'll just have to wait and see. If it doesn't work for him, we're going to have to do some risky surgery.''

"I know you'll do all you can for him, Ross," she said, resting her hand on his arm.

"Maybe he'll surprise us. It happens." He covered her hand with his and smiled at her. "I'll let you know how he does. I'm just sorry we have to cut the evening short. I was looking forward to that cup of coffee you promised me. Maybe you can give me a rain check?"

A throb of excitement pulsed in her throat as his fingers tightened around hers. There was a question in his eyes. "Any time," she said softly.

"I'd like that. I thought this was a very special day." His glance roved over her face, searching, looking deeply into her eyes. Whatever he saw seemed to satisfy him, and his arms slid around her, pulling her close to him. Tilting her chin, he brushed her lips with his. Lightly at first, then as her lips responded to his, claiming them in a long, sweet kiss.

Amanda's heart was pounding when he released her at last. She looked at him wide-eyed, finding no words to express her feelings.

He seemed to be under the same spell. "You know, I think you and I might be working on something special," he said with an appealing smile that set her senses clamoring. "Think about it."

His lips touched hers in a last, gentle kiss, and he was gone, leaving her shaken and breathless. While her tumultuous emotions subsided, she relived the experiences of the lovely day. Ross was a totally surprising man with a devastating masculine charm, a man who was very different from the intense, pragmatic doctor she saw at the hospital. He was an intriguing person with unexpected facets to his personality, a person with an amazing range of interests, a wonderful sense of humor, and a sincere concern for people. Ross was a very special man indeed—so special, Amanda realized with sudden astonishing clarity, that she was dangerously close to falling in love with him.

Chapter Eight

Amanda awoke on Sunday morning to the patter of raindrops on her bedroom window. In its capricious way, October had changed its appearance overnight. In contrast to the sunshine of the day before, it now brought a steady rainfall and the first chill of fall. She snuggled deeper beneath the covers. It was a luxury to sleep in on a rainy Sunday morning.

She lay awake, reliving the events of the previous day. Thinking of Ross, remembering his strong profile silhouetted in the setting sun, his teasing smile, the special way he had looked at her, the way he had kissed her, she sighed dreamily.

Her thoughts turned to Billy Ray Johnson. Ross had left no doubt that he was in grave condition, and she wondered with concern what had happened during the night. She thought of Kitty, and her heart went out to the frightened young wife who waited, hoping for the miracle of healing that seemed so elusive. Yet she found reassurance in knowing Ross was looking after Billy Ray. If anybody could help him, Ross would do it.

As the realities of the day intruded upon her dreamy reverie, Amanda recalled that she had promised to meet her friend Liza for lunch. In spite of the rain, she decided to keep the appointment. Connie would be at her parents' home until after dinner that night, and there was little appeal in a day spent alone in the apartment.

Liza was as willing as she was to brave the weather, and they went on with the outing they had planned. Their day turned out to be a surprisingly pleasant one. It was always good to spend time with someone whose life didn't center on the hospital. Liza, who worked as a computer programmer, brought an interesting glimpse of the business world. After lunch at a favorite restaurant, they went on to a new movie that both of them had wanted to see. By the time Amanda returned to the apartment, it was late afternoon.

Connie telephoned to say she would be late, so Amanda had the apartment to herself. Relaxed and in cheerful spirits, she attacked the weekend duties she had so far neglected. It would be a good time to do laundry and a bit of cleaning. She pulled her hair back behind a headband, slipped into jeans and a baggy T-shirt, and turned up the stereo and set to work.

It was almost eight o'clock by the time she put the cleaning supplies away and folded the last load of laundry. She sank down on the living-room sofa, tired but satisfied. Brushing the dust from her shirt and kicking off her sneakers, she settled down to enjoy the peanut-butter sandwich she had made for supper.

When the doorbell rang, she answered it with a trace of annoyance. Disheveled as she was, she was in no mood to have unannounced company. When she opened the door, she stepped back in surprise. Lounging against the doorframe, smiling down at her, was Tony Lawrence.

Even the rain couldn't dampen Tony's sartorial perfection. He looked more handsome than usual, wearing a stylish trench coat over pleated slacks and a pullover sweater. His hair glistened with the sparkle of raindrops, and his dark eyes held a glint of amusement as he smiled down at Amanda. "Hi, gorgeous. The bad penny has turned up as promised. I told you I'd be around to see you."

Without waiting to be invited, he entered the apartment, nodding approvingly as he glanced around the living room. "A very cozy, tidy place that suits you exactly—although I should have thought you deserved a better supper than a peanut-butter sandwich.''

"I like peanut butter," Amanda retorted.

"Probably mixed with some inedible combination like mashed banana," he commented as he leaned down to inspect her sandwich.

"Marshmallow cream," she corrected him.

"An even more unappetizing combination. I must say, though, that peanut butter looks good on you." With the tip of his finger, he wiped a small blob of peanut butter from the corner of her mouth. Licking the peanut butter from his finger, he nodded approvingly. "Surprisingly good, but somehow I don't think it's the peanut butter. It's the flavoring. You really do have luscious-looking lips, Amanda.''

She hastily reached for a napkin to wipe her mouth. He leaned forward to brush his fingers across the end of her nose. "I also love a turned-up nose," he observed, "even when it's got a streak of dust on it.''

"I really wasn't expecting company, you know," she said, exasperated.

"Actually, I've been looking forward to seeing the real you. And I must say I like this Amanda much better than the efficient, professional Ms. Summers.''

Amanda's annoyance erupted. It was just like this arrogant man to appear unannounced and make himself at home. "I'm not used to having former patients show up at my apartment uninvited. How did you find out where I live?" she demanded.

"Oh, I have my sources. And you can't say you weren't forewarned. I told you I'd be around to see you when I recovered."

He pointed to his throat to indicate the absence of a neck brace. Amanda wondered if Ross knew he had abandoned it. "Has Dr. McKinnon released you?" she asked.

"Except for periodic checkups, he's through with me. Literally. And I must say that he's as happy to be rid of me as I am to be rid of him."

"Dr. McKinnon is a very good doctor." Amanda's voice held a note of reproach.

"Of course he is. That's why I retained him. If somebody is going to be poking around my spinal cord, I want the nimblest fingers available." He leaned back against the sofa and smiled at her in amusement. "You don't have to defend Dr. McKinnon to me. He's a fine neurosurgeon, and I'm well aware that he did a very good piece of work on me. I may be an annoying patient, but I'm not a fool. I don't have any more desire to spend my life in a wheelchair than anyone else."

"I'm glad to hear that. For a while I wondered."

"Wonder no more. I'm being very sensible about myself—to a point, that is. A man has to have a little spice in his life. As a matter of fact, that's why I'm here. I'm laying the groundwork for our future relationship. I have plans for us.''

Amanda decided the time had come to be blunt with this man. He was no longer her patient, and she had no professional obligation to him. He was now on her turf, and she could meet him on her own terms. ''I don't see any kind of relationship between us,'' she said, regarding him coldly. ''You and I move in separate worlds and have totally different ideas and values.''

''You don't know that. You know nothing of my values, and you won't know any of my ideas until you let me explain them to you. That's why I'm here. I'm putting in my bid for a small share of your time and a chance to make my case. I find you intriguing, and I'd like to get to know you better.''

She shook her head firmly. ''Because you're bored and looking for something to occupy you, I appear to be new and different. And, frankly, I don't want to be a diversion. Even if I were willing, it would be a waste of time for both of us.''

''It's never a waste of time to explore a potential relationship,'' he said, unperturbed. ''How else can you know what you might be missing?''

''In our case, I don't think that's an issue. You and I have nothing in common, Tony.''

He grinned mischievously, dismissing her ob- jection. ''That's where you're mistaken. However,

I won't press my luck. For now, we've come along well enough. But I warn you I've only begun. I'm going to prove to you that we have a great deal more in common than you think.''

Amanda glared at him. ''I don't think so.''

''Why don't we just wait and see? I know better, of course, than to try to change your mind tonight. But I'm not giving up. I'm a patient man.''

Her temper flared. ''You're a destructive man, and I have no wish to be involved with you. I'm not an object to be used for your amusement. Do us both a favor and don't come back.''

He merely smiled. ''You're wrong about me. You're also wrong about us. And I intend to prove it to you.'' Without warning, he bent down to brush her lips with a quick, teasing kiss. ''Good night for now.''

Without waiting for her response, he was out the door and gone, leaving her speechless with astonishment. *The nerve of the man!* she told herself indignantly as she dumped her uneaten sandwich in the kitchen disposal. Thanks to him, she no longer had the slightest appetite.

Disgruntled, she took a warm, soothing shower and got ready for bed, but it was some time before she fell asleep, incensed as she was by Tony's audacity. She couldn't believe he had actually showed up at her home. If he came around again, she would slam the door in his face.

She had always drawn a sharp line between the patients she worked with at the hospital and the people she dealt with in her private life. Otherwise, it would be impossible to maintain the objectivity her job required. Empathetic as she might be with the people she tried to help, she couldn't let herself become involved in their personal problems. To do so would interfere with the clarity of judgment and impartiality that a counselor needed to do an effective job.

Tony definitely wasn't a person to become involved with. He had been a difficult patient, so he would be an even more troublesome person to deal with socially. He thrived on confrontation and living on the edge; he invited danger and controversy. Since she wanted no part of either, she didn't intend to let him bring them into her life.

It wasn't until her indignation had cooled that she was able to think of other, more interesting subjects, like the pleasant day she had spent with Ross. Dreamily, she thought back over the happy moments she had shared with him, reliving them once again.

She wondered what he had done that day and if all had gone well for Billy Ray. She was drifting off to sleep before she remembered that Ross hadn't telephoned her as he had promised.

Chapter Nine

Amanda arrived at her office the next morning, hoping to find a message from Ross. Instead, she found a memo on her desk requesting her to report to Tom Franklin, head of Social Services. Tom had an assignment for her. He had been scheduled to go to Chicago for a week-long meeting, but a conflict had developed in his schedule. Unexpected hospital business was forcing him to skip the meeting, and he wanted Amanda to fill in for him.

"You'll need to leave early this afternoon," he explained. "I know it's short notice, but I think you'll find it worth the effort. There'll be some top-ranking people there. Frankly, I'm very disappointed that I'm not going."

Amanda was excited about the trip. It was a

compliment to be chosen to replace Tom, and a fine opportunity to hear some of the newest ideas in their field of work. "I can make it," she assured Tom.

"Be sure and bring back all the information you can so we can share it with the others in the department," he said.

The rest of the morning was a race against time. Amanda attended to what business she could, and Tom arranged with the other counselors to cover her assignments during the coming week. By mid-morning she was ready to leave the hospital and pack for the trip.

Only as she left the department was she reminded that there still had been no message from Ross and no news of Billy Ray. Concerned, she wondered about how he had fared since Saturday night.

Reluctant to leave the hospital without news, she made a quick trip to NICU on her way out of the hospital. At the desk, she learned that Billy Ray was still holding his own without surgery. Kitty was nowhere to be seen. Apparently, she was keeping vigil in his hospital room.

She didn't see Ross, either. He seemed to be lost somewhere in the remote world between surgery and intensive care, where he couldn't be reached. Amanda left the hospital feeling disappointed. She would have liked to talk to Ross before she left town, but it would have been presumptuous to page him and awkward to leave a message with his assistant. She sighed. Ross was back in his isolated professional arena, detached and unapproachable.

As she went home and packed for her trip, Amanda couldn't help feeling rejected. It was almost as if her lovely Saturday with Ross had never happened.

Personal problems had to be put aside, however, during the busy week of meetings that followed. The conference was all that Tom had promised, and the week proved to be well spent. Amanda returned from the seminar on Friday afternoon with a wealth of information to share with her colleagues.

She dropped off her suitcase at the apartment and hurried to the hospital to check on developments there. A week was a long time to be away from the busy department, and there was sure to be a great deal of catching up to do. She didn't want to go into the weekend without finding out what had happened during her absence.

In her office, she shuffled hastily through an accumulation of memos and telephone messages, expecting to find a message from Ross. To her disappointment, there was nothing. Nor was there any news of Billy Ray. No one else in the department had been following his progress while she was away. A call to NICU revealed only that his condition was stable.

Before she left the hospital that evening, she stopped by NICU to check on Billy Ray. Kitty was waiting in her customary spot. She revealed that Billy Ray, though disoriented, was conscious. "Dr. McKinnon says he's holding his own," she reported. "They changed his medicine, and he seems able to stay awake more."

Amanda went home, relieved for the Johnsons but puzzled by the silence from Ross. She had expected to hear something from him during the week, if for no other reason than to give her a report on Billy Ray.

That evening, when Connie told her that Ross hadn't called her at the apartment, her disappointment began to turn into hurt feelings. It appeared that she had been mistaken about his interest in her. Apparently, she had misconstrued the things he had said. While the lovely Saturday they had spent together had been special to her, it seemed to have meant nothing to him. Already he had forgotten it.

In disillusionment, she unpacked her suitcase and changed into jeans and a pullover. She had started toward the kitchen to put together something for supper when the doorbell rang. Connie, who was expecting a friend to stop by, answered the door.

"I must say you're the last person I'd expect to see," she exclaimed as she stepped back to admit the caller. "You can't possibly want to see me, given our adversarial relationship, so you must have come to see Amanda.''

''I'd never characterize our relationship in those terms,'' an amused male voice replied. ''Believe me, I have all the respect in the world for you and your professional dedication. It's just that I've become fascinated by your beautiful roommate.''

With dismay, Amanda recognized Tony's voice. What was it going to take to discourage this man? She set down the peanut butter and marshmallow cream sandwich she was assembling and started from the kitchen, determined to set him straight.

Connie met her in the doorway, her brown eyes round with surprise. ''Wow!'' she whispered. ''Why didn't you tell me you and Tony Terrific had something going?''

''We don't. He's just having a little trouble getting the message.'' Amanda set her chin in determination. ''I guess I'm going to have to find a way to get through to him.''

Brushing past Connie, she went into the living room to confront Tony. He didn't give her a chance to speak. ''I see that you're annoyed with me. I seem to keep interrupting your dinner. Peanut butter and marshmallow sandwiches again,'' he observed.

''I like them,'' she said. ''That is, of course, when I can eat them without being disturbed.''

''To each his own taste. Mine runs to steak and

lobster,'' he said, ignoring her pointed remark.
''As a matter of fact, that's why I'm here. I came
to invite you to the Polo Club next Sunday—for
the polo match and dinner afterward. I think I told
you I had my ponies moved to the club here.
They're ready to play, and so am I.''

''I hope you're not thinking of playing polo,''
Connie spoke up. She had joined them in the living
room and was listening to their conversation.

''That depends.'' Tony smiled wickedly at
Amanda. ''With your roommate's entertaining
company, I'd be perfectly happy to be a spectator.
If I were bored and abandoned, however, I'm not
sure I could resist the temptation to climb on a
horse and join the pack. Polo holds a compelling
attraction once the competition gets in your blood.''

''It's also a good way to break your neck—particularly one that's as fragile as yours,'' Connie
said.

He shrugged. ''I might be lucky and break an
arm instead.''

''If you're foolish enough to take the risk, I guess
you won't try to be selective,'' Connie snapped.

''But that's my whole point in coming here. I'm
sincerely trying to resist temptation.'' He glanced
at Amanda. ''I'm hoping you'll come along to keep
me company and save me from myself.''

Amanda met his gaze steadily. ''I told you before
that I'm not an object for you to amuse yourself

with, Tony. And I'm not a crutch for you to lean on, either. Whatever you decide to do, the decision is your responsibility. If you're foolish enough to risk another serious injury, you'll be the one to deal with the consequences, not me.''

A flicker of emotion appeared briefly in Tony's eyes. Rejection, displeasure, fear? Amanda couldn't say. But she knew that, behind his carefree facade, he was still suffering from emotional problems. After all, he was going through an upheaval in the structure of his life.

Still, her understanding of Tony couldn't influence her decision. At this point, it would do him no good for someone else to shoulder his burdens. Making the emotional adjustments he faced was a problem he had to handle alone.

They stood, Tony measuring Amanda, she firmly prepared to resist any entreaty he might make. Connie looked from one to the other of them uncertainly. When the silence was broken by the ring of the doorbell, Amanda turned in relief to answer it.

She pulled the door open abruptly, expecting to see Connie's friend. Instead, Ross stood outside in the hallway.

Amanda was speechless with astonishment. Ross was the last person in the world she expected to see. In her confusion, she could only stare at him.

Connie's eyes widened at the sight of Ross, but quickly she jumped in to take charge of the awkward scene. "Dr. McKinnon, it's nice to see you," she said. "Please come in."

Ross stepped inside but hesitated beside the door as his glance settled on Tony. "Mr. Lawrence," he said in a cool, professional tone.

"It's good to see you, Dr. McKinnon," Tony replied with a level smile. "One would think we were having a reunion of my rehab team. Except that I'm not here on medical business, of course. Having moved on from my patient status, my business is of a social nature." He moved to Amanda's side and rested a hand on her shoulder. "I came to invite Amanda to the polo matches."

"I see." If Ross noticed the possessive gesture, his expression gave no hint. His voice was detached and emotionless as he said, "Then I've come at a bad time."

"Not at all," Tony said smoothly. "Amanda and I have all evening to talk about our plans. But as long as you're here, I'll take advantage of the opportunity to seek your professional advice. Amanda and Connie and I are having a difference of opinion. They seem to think I'm not ready to play polo. What do you think?"

"I think I made that very clear at your last checkup," Ross replied. "But if you want a review of your case, you can come by the office whenever you like. I'll be glad to go over your X rays with you again."

He dismissed the subject by turning to Amanda, who had wriggled out of Tony's grasp. "I won't intrude on your evening, Ms. Summers. I stopped by to tell you that Billy Ray is doing well under the circumstances. I thought you'd want to know since you've taken an interest in his wife."

"I saw Kitty this afternoon," Amanda said quickly. "I was anxious to know how Billy Ray was doing. I've been out of town all week."

"I see." Ross's gaze became even colder. "Then I'm sure you've got catching up to do, so I'll leave you to it." With a glance of dismissal at Tony and a nod to Connie, he left the apartment, closing the door decisively behind him.

Tony gazed at the closed door for a moment and then gave Amanda a critical glance. "You know, Dr. Doom is a dour sort of man. Much too demanding, in my opinion. I suppose it comes with the work."

"He doesn't always get the easiest patients to deal with," Connie said pointedly.

Tony shrugged, dismissing the subject, and turned to Amanda. "The doctor had a point, though, about letting you get on with whatever you have to do. If you've been out of town all week, I'm sure you have things to catch up on. So I'll just leave you to it."

"That would be considerate of you," Amanda

said sarcastically, barely able to speak in her anger.

He smiled at her. "Unlike the doctor, I'm not a demanding man. I won't press you about the polo games. Obviously, you need time to get back on track. I'll be in touch later in the week after you've had a chance to see what your schedule is going to be."

"I already know what it's going to be," she said through clenched teeth. "Thank you for your invitation, but I'm going to decline."

Tony laughed, undaunted. "Why don't we wait and see how your week goes? You may change your mind."

She shook her head with finality. "I don't think so."

"Still, I'll be in touch. As I've said before, I'm a patient man." With an ingratiating smile at Amanda and a polite good night to Connie, he left the apartment.

After he had gone, Connie turned to Amanda, her eyes wide with curiosity. "Would you tell me what's going on? Unless I miss my guess, Ross McKinnon was one ticked-off man."

But Amanda could only shake her head, sick at heart. Whatever was going on with Ross definitely wasn't going on anymore. The distant tone in which he'd called her Ms. Summers made it clear that any personal relationship between them no longer existed. The cold, dispassionate way he had looked at her told her that any affection he might once have had for her was no more.

Chapter Ten

Friday's unhappy events were the forerunner of a gloomy weekend marked by a dreary, unending rain. By Monday, the rain had settled into a dispiriting drizzle that brought the chill of fall to the city.

The disheartening effect of the weather was evident at the hospital in the dispositions of both patients and staff. During her years of teaching music to children, Amanda's mother had always said that rainy days were certain to produce fidgety, uncooperative students. This certainly held true at the hospital. Patients were querulous and restless, trying the patience of the always-pressured staff members.

To add to the depressing atmosphere, Amanda

was confronted with the accumulated fallout from the unattended business of the previous week. Surveying the clutter of papers on her desk, she had to sympathize with the doctors who complained about the never-ending stream of medical forms. Everything needed to be done in triplicate and required a signature.

The thought of unhappy doctors brought up the specter of her disastrous encounter with a certain unfathomable neurosurgeon on Friday night. Ross couldn't possibly have chosen a worse time to stop by her apartment. Thanks to Tony, he had gotten a totally wrong idea and was probably now convinced that she was not only going out with Tony but also encouraging him in his foolhardy pursuits.

Of course, if Ross's silence was any measure, it didn't matter to him what she did in her spare time. As a doctor, however, he wouldn't take kindly to a staff member affecting a patient's program of recovery. She sighed disconsolately. Ross was a total enigma to her. Why did she have to be so deeply attracted to *him?*

And she was more than attracted. If she were honest, she'd have to admit that she was teetering on the edge of falling in love with him. Irascible, contradictory, unpredictable man that he was, he stirred her emotions in a way no one else ever had.

She contemplated her hopeless situation forlornly. Her impossible dreams of Ross were nothing more than a foolish fantasy. Attractive, sought-after bachelors such as he had far too many appealing women to choose from to be interested in an unexceptional counselor like her. Perhaps it was just as well that Friday's encounter had turned out as it had.

In the meantime, there was a mountain of paperwork on her desk waiting to be dealt with. This was no morning to waste in idle speculation about a man who could cause her nothing but heartache. Determinedly, Amanda sat down at her desk and attacked the morning's work.

Deep in concentration, she paid no attention to the traffic in and out of the room. There was always a steady procession of people through the Social Services office, and she had long ago learned to ignore the distractions. Only vaguely did she become aware that someone was standing by her desk. "Excuse me," a voice repeated. "Can I speak to you for a moment, Ms. Summers?"

Amanda looked up from her work to see an attractive young woman observing her intently. "I'm sorry. I didn't see you come in," she apologized.

"I should have called for an appointment, but I took a chance and stopped by your office. I hope you don't mind. I'm Erica Danforth, and I've come to talk to you about Tony Lawrence. He's a friend of mine."

Erica managed an impressively stylish appearance, even on this soggy day. She wore an attractive yellow raincoat and knee-high boots. Her copper-colored hair was cut in a short, gamin style that was only enhanced by the raindrops that dampened it. A colorful scarf at her throat brought out the tawny lights in her hair and complemented the amber color of her wide, intelligent eyes. Gold hoop earrings accented aristocratically molded features and a direct, inquiring regard. She gave the immediate impression of a self-assured woman who knew what she wanted and was used to getting it.

The question for Amanda, of course, was what Erica wanted. Amanda offered her the chair that was drawn up in front of her desk and put down her pen. "I'll be glad to help you however I can, but I don't have any connection with Tony since he's no longer a patient at the hospital," she explained.

Erica brushed her explanation aside with a quick smile. "Frankly, I realize I'm intruding on you— as well as on Tony. But Tony is my friend, and I do care what he does to himself. I was hoping you might help me keep him from killing himself."

Amanda's interest was captured by the candid words as well as by Erica's frank, engaging expression. "I can certainly appreciate your concern for Tony. He hasn't been the most realistic patient."

"I know, and that's why I've come to you. Tony is admittedly an egotistical man who's used to doing as he pleases, but behind the arrogance there's a very special person. He's not nearly as inconsiderate as he seems, nor is he as nonchalant about his problems as he wants to appear. He's actually feeling quite threatened and insecure. Right now, Tony is going through a very bad time, and I'm willing to go to whatever lengths I have to in order to help him."

"You're very perceptive," Amanda said. "He's faced with some changes in his life that threaten his self-image, and this is very difficult for him to deal with."

"Tony isn't willing to change. That's why I'm here."

"You know, of course, that I'm not free to discuss his case with anyone without his permission."

"I don't expect you to. Tony has told me about the advice he received from his doctor and the professionals who have worked with him, and I know that he was advised to seek counseling to help him deal with the emotional impact of his accident. That's what I want your help with."

"He refused to accept counseling. Under the circumstances, it wouldn't be proper for me to approach him. To be honest, though, I don't think there's a way in the world I can help with Tony."

"But there is. You see, he's totally infatuated with you."

"Right now I'm a diversion for him," Amanda

objected. "Believe me, it isn't unusual for patients to attach themselves emotionally to a therapist, although it's usually someone they've worked more closely with than Tony and I did. In Tony's case, I think the fact that I'm a nonmedical and non-threatening figure makes me seem more understanding to him. I capture his interest. As he gets back into his own life, the infatuation will pass. It always does."

"I think you're right," Erica agreed. "And after meeting you, I'm sure you'll help him keep a healthy perspective. Of course, I had no way of knowing whether you might be interested in Tony. But seeing that your interest in him is totally professional, I feel even better about coming to you. You see, I'm going to ask a favor of you that I hope you'll consider."

"I don't understand," Amanda said, puzzled.

"It's about the polo match next Sunday. Tony told me that he had invited you, and I'm hoping you'll accept his invitation."

Amanda frowned. "I can't. It would be misleading to him and would create problems for me that I really don't want to deal with."

"Then come as *my* guest." When Amanda shook her head, Erica persisted. "Hear me out at least. You see, Tony isn't just a spoiled boy. He's a complex man who, in spite of his wealth, hasn't had the easiest time of it. His mother died when he was only six, and his father was a semi-invalid during the last years of his life. He centered all his affection on Tony, sharing all his business and personal problems, and without realizing it shifted them to his son. By the time Tony was in high school, he was serving as his father's spokesman in business matters. He was only twenty-one and just out of college when his father died and he had to assume the responsibilities of a man twice his age."

Erica shook her head regretfully as she continued her narrative. "The result was Tony never really had a youth, and grew up with a dread of illness and old age. He hung in there until his dad died, but afterward he reacted by plunging into daring pursuits, defying misfortune and death. I think maybe he's subconsciously challenging fate."

"It would be an understandable reaction. He's fortunate to have such a perceptive and caring friend," Amanda said, touched by Tony's story.

"I've known him since we were kids, and he's always been there for me," Erica explained. "When I married much too young, Tony helped me pick up the pieces after the marriage failed. Without him, I don't know where I would be now. In any event, it's my turn to help him. I care about him, and I'm willing to do anything to help him get through this."

"You'll need a lot of patience," Amanda warned.

"I know. Tony doesn't like the thought of needing help from anyone. He refused to have visitors here at the hospital and even ordered me not to come. I understood. He didn't want anyone to see his weakness."

"That's not an unusual reaction."

"I understand that, and I also know Tony well enough to know better than to tell him what to do. But I'm going to do my best to help him in spite of himself. I want to get him interested in something to replace his more dangerous hobbies."

"I've wondered why a successful businessman like Tony isn't more interested in his business affairs," Amanda commented. "Most people would find that challenging enough."

"The challenge for Tony is in organizing an operation and making it a success. He has good people running his enterprises for him and is smart enough not to interfere with them. Also, he wants to move on to something different. His real interest now is breeding and training his polo ponies. He has a trainer to work with them and ride them, and I'm convinced he plays in the matches occasionally only because he feels it's expected of him. I think he really prefers to watch his horses perform rather than to ride them. What I'm hoping is that he'll build on this interest and get involved from a spectator point of view.''

''It sounds like a promising outlet for him,'' Amanda agreed.

''If he can get past this feeling that he has to compete, I think he'll discover that he can get a lot of satisfaction out of promoting the sport and his horse farm. That's why I've come to you. Please come to the match and let him show off his ponies and the polo club to you. Your opinion of him is important. If he sees that you approve of what he's doing, maybe he can make the transition from contestant to sponsor.''

''I'm not prepared to be a crutch for him.''

''Neither am I. I'm only trying to point him in the right direction. He has to do the rest himself.''

''But I have a life of my own, and, frankly, I don't want Tony involved in it,'' Amanda said.

''Then tell him so—after you've given him your approval. Right now, you've become Tony's challenge. The harder you resist him, the more determined he'll be to succeed with you. But he isn't a fool. If he sees that you're willing to be a friend and nothing more, he'll settle for your friendship.''

''I've always made it a policy not to get involved with patients. In the long run, it doesn't work for anybody,'' Amanda said doubtfully.

''Then come to the matches with somebody else. Let me give you tickets. If you're there, it will give

Tony the excuse not to ride. Whether or not he
knows it, that's what he's looking for. He doesn't
want to risk another injury any more than I do. I
think he knows, deep down inside, what he has to
do. He's just not ready to admit it.''

''I hope he knows what a good friend you are
to him,'' Amanda said, admiring the lengths Erica
was willing to go in the name of friendship.

''He's been a savior to me, and there's very little
I wouldn't do for him in return. I'm even willing
to beg a beautiful woman to give him her attention.''

''That's not hard to do. Tony's a very attractive
man. It's just. . . .'' Amanda paused.

''Is there someone else?''

She shook her head. ''It's just not a good idea
to encourage an involvement that isn't good for
either of us.''

''I can certainly understand how you feel, but
will you at least consider accepting the invitation?''

''Maybe, if it will put an end to this idea of
Tony's. I'm just not convinced that it will.''

''At least think about it.''

Erica left as abruptly as she had come, leaving
Amanda to consider their conversation. Maybe
there was something in what she suggested. At the
very least, it was worth talking to Connie about.
As Tony's physical therapist, Connie would surely
have an opinion. Practical, levelheaded Connie

could always be counted on to see things objec-
tively.

For most of the day, Amanda was able to put
personal problems out of her mind. Her schedule
didn't allow time for brooding. She didn't even
think of Ross until that afternoon, when she visited
a new patient in the neurological wing. The patient,
a man in his early thirties, had undergone surgery
for a brain tumor and was going to require rehabilitation services. Dr. Foster had assigned Amanda
to his rehab team. When the patient's record revealed that Ross had performed the surgery,
Amanda wondered how he would react to her assignment.

She became even more uncertain when, on the
way to the patient's room, she stopped by the
nurse's station to inquire about Billy Ray. Still
curious about Ross's unexpected visit to her apartment the night before to report on Billy Ray, she
wanted to follow up on his report.

She learned that Billy Ray's condition was satisfactory, which meant he was holding his own.
The report left Amanda mystified. Why would Ross
have made a special trip to her apartment to tell
her this?

Of course, she still entertained the feeble hope
that he had come because he wanted to see her.
Then why had he waited so long? He could have

left a message for her at work. He could have telephoned while she was still in town. There were a dozen things he could have done to let her know he was interested in her. His silence had to be accepted for what it was. Either Ross had decided not to pursue a personal interest in her, or, worse, had decided that he really didn't have any.

She sighed unhappily as she turned into the patient's room. Distracted by her thoughts, she didn't notice until she entered the room that a doctor, assisted by Rose O'Bannon, was at the bedside examining the patient. Immediately she identified the doctor's unruly brown hair and broad shoulders.

She was backing out of the room when he glanced up, annoyed by the interruption. His irritation sharpened as he recognized her. "Would you please wait outside, Ms. Summers? I'll talk to you when we're finished here," he said curtly.

There was an authoritative edge to his voice. He had issued a command, not a request. Amanda waited outside the room uneasily.

He came out a short time later, still accompanied by Rose. His eyes were cold as he regarded Amanda. "What business do you have with this patient?" he asked in a clipped, brusque tone.

"Dr. Foster asked me to do a workup on the social services he'll need."

"At present, the patient isn't in any condition to be concerned about social services, and I don't want you taxing him with questions. You'll have to wait until later to fill out your forms.''

There was no mistaking his cutting tone or his derogatory glance at the clipboard she carried. Biting back her hurt feelings, Amanda answered evenly, ''The family has requested certain services that they think the patient is entitled to. I can keep my contact with him as brief as you think necessary, but he has a right to ask for our help. I won't contact him again until we have your permission.''

''See that you don't.''

''Yes, Dr. McKinnon.'' Amanda gritted her teeth in frustration. ''I'll tell Dr. Foster.''

''That won't be necessary. I'll speak to him myself.''

With a nod of dismissal, he turned abruptly and strode off down the hall with Rose trailing silently after him. As she passed, the nurse's face was expressionless except for a lifted eyebrow that told Amanda Dr. McKinnon was being his usual, difficult self.

Amanda's temper erupted. She had done nothing to Ross to cause him to treat her this way. She had given him no reason to find fault with her work. He was a bad-tempered, domineering tyrant of a man, and she had been a fool to let herself think there could ever be a personal relationship between them.

For the rest of the day, she smoldered silently,

but by the time she left the hospital she had made a decision. She didn't intend to have her life muddied by a man who had no regard for her feelings. Not Ross McKinnon, and not Tony Lawrence. Starting now, she intended to rid herself of both of them. She would keep a safe distance from Ross, and she would immediately put a stop to Tony's intrusion in her life. She even had thought of a way to do it. When Tony called about the polo match, she knew exactly what she was going to do—provided she could persuade Connie to go along with her plan.

Chapter Eleven

The polo match at Woody Hollow Polo Club turned out to be an exciting event. Sitting with Tony and Erica, Amanda and Connie were at once caught up in the excitement of the game. The daring and skill of the riders combined with the speed and strength of the tough little horses was thrilling to watch.

Amanda's plan had worked out even better than she had hoped. With Connie's cooperation, she had arranged for the two of them to meet Tony at the polo field. By including Connie, she made it clear that accepting his invitation meant she had no romantic interest. Tony had not objected, seeming quite pleased to include Connie. Having never seen a polo match, she had agreed to forgo her usual

weekend visit with her family and accompany
Amanda. Finally, by previous arrangement with
Amanda, Erica materialized from the crowd to join
them.

Tony seemed happy with the arrangement. He
enthusiastically explained the game to Amanda
while Erica, on his other side, talked to Connie.
Tony was particularly proud of his string of horses,
explaining that a player would use several mounts
in the course of the game. The fast pace and hard
riding required a ready supply of fresh horses. Even
with her slight knowledge of horses, Amanda was
impressed by the tough little ponies, which were
chosen for their speed and endurance.

The players were equally impressive. Lean, muscular men with the strength to control the excited
animals, they rode with skill and daring. Players
maneuvered for position, mallets swinging as they
vied for shots. Hooves pounded as a player would
suddenly break loose from the pack, bending low
in the saddle to drive the ball down the field and
race after it at breakneck speed.

Tony's trainer was an excellent rider who handled the horses expertly, and Tony seemed content
to have him ride in his place. It soon became evident that Tony's first interest was in his horses,
and he proudly pointed out the fact that his barns
had supplied two of the ponies being ridden by
other competitors.

Erica explained that Tony operated a horse farm for breeding and training the ponies. The barns produced a fine strain of animals, which were sought after by polo enthusiasts. Clearly, Tony found the operation to be a fascinating pursuit and considered it a challenging business. Watching him, Amanda agreed with Erica that this could well be the outlet Tony needed to direct his interest away from competition.

As the game progressed, Tony turned more and more of his attention to Erica. He explained to Amanda that Erica was an accomplished equestrienne who kept her horses at the Polo Club barns and frequently rode in hunter-jumper competitions. The two of them obviously shared a close, comfortable friendship, and Tony was clearly as proud of Erica's accomplishments as he was of his polo ponies.

By the time the game was over, the foursome had established a comfortable companionship. When they went to the clubhouse for dinner, they were surrounded by friends of Tony's and Erica's who wanted to wish Tony well and express their pleasure at his recovery. It was apparent at once to Amanda and Connie that they had been invited to an important social gathering.

The event, the proceeds from which were to be donated to a homeless shelter in the city, was receiving considerable publicity and was heavily attended. A number of the people present were prominent in city affairs. A photographer and reporter from the local newspaper circulated through the room, snapping pictures and interviewing some of the celebrities. When the reporter approached Tony, seeking a report on his recent accident, Tony was polite but noncommittal, unwilling to invite publicity.

Connie and Amanda stood next to Erica, watching the parade of people who stopped to express their good wishes. "Have you noticed that none of them has mentioned the fact that Tony isn't riding?" Connie commented.

"That's because they care about him," Erica said. "Tony has a lot of friends who'd be happy if he never played a game of polo again. They've been hoping for a long time that he'd give up the race cars and speedboats. He doesn't see it, but they like to be with him simply because he's a great guy."

"I have to confess that I'm seeing a very different person from the patient I worked with," Connie said.

"Tony's a very special man. People have no idea of the many good things he does. He sponsors a sports center for fatherless boys, for instance. The staff there does wonderful work with troubled kids who have nowhere to go but the streets." Erica smiled proudly. "Of course, you mustn't let Tony know that I told you about it. He's very private about his involvement in these projects.''

As Amanda saw the pride in Erica's eyes, she understood that Erica's relationship with Tony was based on much more than friendship. It was plain to see Erica was in love with him. The two of them made a striking couple, she with her tawny, sophisticated beauty and he with his dark good looks. During dinner, listening to the friendly banter between them, Amanda could only marvel that Tony hadn't seen long ago that this was the woman for him.

Whatever he saw or felt, Tony was a perfect host. He divided his attention evenly among his three companions and went out of his way to be entertaining. As the evening progressed and he continued to display none of the irritating boldness he had shown toward Amanda in the past, she was able to relax and enjoy his company.

He didn't object when, after dinner, Amanda and Connie got ready to leave. While he accompanied them to the door, he didn't offer to drive Amanda home. He did, however, extend an invitation to future games. ''You'll make first-class polo fans,'' he told them.

''I'm already a fan,'' Amanda assured him.

''This was really fun,'' Connie added. ''It was nice of you to include me.''

''My pleasure,'' he said graciously. ''It's a small

token in exchange for your putting up with me over the last few weeks.''

Connie grinned. ''You really were a pain.''

''And you're painfully honest. I hope you won't be disappointed to know that I'm increasing my outpatient therapy schedule. You're going to be seeing me three times a week.''

''You may change your mind when you see how I'm going to work you,'' Connie teased. ''I can be merciless.''

''So can I,'' Tony said. ''Before we're through, you may be begging me to let up on you.''

While his tone was light and joking, there was a quiet determination in Tony's eyes. Something had changed his attitude completely.

His treatment of Amanda was puzzling too. While Erica, who had accompanied them to the entrance to the club, spoke with Connie, he pulled Amanda aside to speak to her privately. ''Thanks for coming today. I hope you enjoyed yourself as much as you seemed to.''

''It was great. No wonder you're so proud of your beautiful horses. It was a real thrill to see them in action.''

''Even though I trapped you into accepting my invitation?''

''We came because we wanted to.''

''Thank you for not saying you came because it was part of your job. I'm glad you brought Connie." His incisive glance told her he was aware of her tactics. "You didn't need the protection, though. I may come on a bit strong at times, but I'm harmless. Besides, I got the picture the other night at your apartment."

Amanda smiled. "Then it was especially nice of you to invite me."

He shrugged. "Obviously, I went about it all wrong, but from the beginning all I wanted was for us to get to know each other better. And I think we have. You see, even if you can offer me nothing but your friendship, I value that. You've helped me see some things about myself, and I'm very grateful."

"I'd like to be your friend too. You really are a nice man."

He threw back his head and laughed, his white teeth flashing and a glint of mischief dancing in his eyes. "I think this is the first time a woman has told me I'm a nice man. I don't know whether that's a compliment or a rejection." He reached out to touch Erica's arm and draw her close to him. "Did you hear what she said, Erica? She has totally destroyed my image. This is what happens when a man gets himself mixed up with a psychologist."

"Actually, she's quite right. Whether you like to admit it or not, you really are a nice man. You're the best friend anyone could ever have," Erica said. She held out her hand to Amanda. "I'd like to add my invitation to Tony's. Please come to the matches again.''

With her arm linked through his, Erica stood beside Tony while they said good night. They stood close together, watching their guests depart.

''I don't know what's happened to Tony, but he's a totally different person,'' Connie said thoughtfully while they were driving home. ''Maybe now that he's out of the hospital and back in his own world, he's seen how lucky he was to survive such a terrible accident.''

''I think he's known it all along but just couldn't admit it. What's happened to Tony is Erica. She's helped him see his life from a different perspective. I just hope he realizes how lucky he is to have someone like her.''

Connie nodded. ''So do I, because she's obviously in love with him. She's the best thing that could possibly happen to him.''

''Maybe Tony will figure that out,'' Amanda said. ''If he's smart enough to include Erica in his future plans, I think there will be some pretty wonderful things in his life.''

At the meeting of the rehab team the following week, Connie was able to report a completely changed attitude on Tony's part in his first two sessions of physical therapy. Encouraged by the report, Amanda was optimistic about his total recovery. Maybe he was finally getting realistic about himself.

The meeting was almost over when Ross entered the room and positioned himself near the door. He had come to cover the workup on a patient who had just been assigned to the rehab program. His comments were brief and succinct, and the meeting broke up shortly afterward.

Amanda lingered, waiting for him to leave, feeling awkward about speaking to him after their last, unpleasant meeting. However, he stood leaning against the door while the rest of the team filed past him. Having no other recourse, Amanda followed, nodding politely to him as she approached.

"If you can spare the time, I'd like to talk to you," he said, his blue eyes icy cold. "As you know, I believe in being open with the people I work with. As long as you're going to be dealing with patients of mine, I think we ought to have an understanding."

Amanda was taken aback by his angry tone. Unquestionably, she was going to receive a dressing-down. The problem was, she had no idea what she had done to displease him.

She met his disapproval as coolly as she could manage. "I believe in being open too. If there's something you think needs to be said, I'd like to hear it."

"Okay. I have questions about your approach to

your work. I thought you were much more professional.''

"Maybe you'd better tell me what you consider
to be unprofessional.''

He took a folded newspaper clipping from his
pocket and thrust it at her. "I was surprised to see
this in the morning paper.''

She saw that the photograph apparently had been
taken at Sunday's polo match. It showed Tony
looking down at her and holding her hand while
she smiled up at him attentively.

"I don't understand,'' she said in confusion,
trying to recall when the picture might have been
taken. She had certainly not posed for any photograph with Tony.

"I think it's pretty clear. Of course, I'm not
surprised at Tony, because the man has demon-
strated over and over that he's a fool. But I did
expect better of you.''

Bewildered, Amanda tried to make sense of
Ross's accusations. Studying the newspaper clipping more closely, she noticed the caption beneath
the picture: *Millionaire sportsman Tony Lawrence,
recovered from his recent race-car accident, cel-
ebrates his return to polo competition during the
games on Sunday at Woody Hollow Polo Club.*

"But . . .'' Amanda protested, baffled by the
caption. She had certainly not been aware of any
such announcement. She remembered Tony talking

to a reporter, but he had said nothing to her or Connie about planning to return to competition.

Ross didn't wait for her to finish. "If the man is determined to destroy himself, it's his own business, but I didn't think you'd encourage him. Apparently, I misjudged you."

"Now, wait a minute—"

"I know that what you say and what you do don't always match up. You talk about your commitment to your work, but you don't seem to back it up."

"This picture gives a totally false impression. Just because I was at the polo match doesn't mean—"

He interrupted her explanation. "Obviously, it's not my business what you do in your spare time. But your attitude toward my patients *is* my business. I won't stand by without comment when I see you encouraging this man to play polo when you know he could harm himself."

"If you'll let me explain—" Amanda protested.

"I think it's very clear, and I'm sure the two of you had an exciting afternoon. I just hope you're still around when Tony paralyzes himself."

Before Amanda could reply, he turned away and strode off without looking back. She stood, looking down at the newspaper clipping in her hand, bewildered. The longer she looked at it, the angrier she became. Once again, Ross had jumped to his own conclusions without waiting to hear the facts.

It was pointless to try to mend their misunderstanding. There was no possibility of any kind of relationship between them. The way things stood now, there was no longer any hope that they could even be friends.

Chapter Twelve

"I just don't understand it," Amanda said to Connie that evening at their apartment while they shared a supper of soup and salad. "I don't remember ever posing for a picture with Tony—much less this one."

They sat at the dining room table, turning through the morning paper, which neither of them had seen until now. Amanda was searching the sports section for local polo news while Connie read the society page where the picture of Tony and Amanda had appeared.

Connie studied the picture once again, carefully reading the caption. "I remember the photographer moving through the crowd all evening. He must have taken this one without your knowing it."

"But I don't remember ever being alone with Tony. Except . . ." Amanda thought back to the moment just before they had left the club, when Tony had teased her about bringing Connie along for protection. "Just before we left, he drew me aside. I suppose the picture could have been taken then."

Connie nodded and handed the newspaper to Amanda. "I still don't understand this caption, though. This sounds as if Tony played in the matches Sunday, and he didn't."

"Has he mentioned anything during his therapy sessions that would lead you to think he's considering playing?"

"If he did, I certainly didn't hear it. I don't think he's even mentioned polo."

Amanda shook her head, mystified. "I can't imagine where the newspaper reporter got the idea Tony played last Sunday."

"Maybe it was just a misquote," Connie suggested. "That happens, you know."

"I wish you'd tell that to Ross," Amanda said bitterly. "The way he has it figured out, Tony was galloping up and down the polo field with me standing on the sidelines cheering."

"It was that bad?"

"Worse. He didn't even give me a chance to explain. He just walked off in a huff before I could say a word."

Connie cast a speculative glance at Amanda. "Has it occurred to you that maybe Ross doesn't much like the idea of you and Tony hanging out together?"

"Ross has made it clear that he doesn't much like anything about me."

"Somehow I don't get that impression."

"That's because you didn't hear him chew me out. He's convinced that I'm totally irresponsible, and I doubt there's anything I can do to change his mind."

"I wouldn't be too sure about that," Connie said with a knowing smile. "Why don't we just wait and see what happens?"

As it turned out, there was little to wait for and nothing at all to see. Ross's patients didn't need Amanda's services all week, nor did she see him. He seemed to be staying out of her way.

She spent a lonely weekend at the apartment while Connie paid her customary visit to her parents. She used the time to good advantage, attending to household chores, catching up on her reading, and nursing her bruised feelings. Although she tried to put the misunderstanding with Ross out of her mind, it still hurt to recall his unjust accusations. At least he could have listened to her explanation.

The weekend also passed without further news

of Tony, as did the following week. Connie reported that he was dedicated to his program of therapy but had made no mention of his private life. They decided that he was occupied, as he should be, with his own affairs. Their brief involvement with him was over, and he had moved on with his life.

Late in the week, Amanda received a disturbing call concerning Billy Ray Johnson. He had taken a sudden turn for the worse and was undergoing emergency surgery. Kitty was asking for her.

In view of Ross's disapproving attitude toward her, Amanda was hesitant to approach one of his patients. Still, she couldn't ignore the request. Deciding that her duty had to come before personal disagreements, she set out for the waiting room on the surgical floor.

She found Kitty sitting anxiously in a corner. Her eyes were frightened and red-rimmed from weeping. "Billy Ray's really bad this time," she said as Amanda sat down beside her. "They may not be able to save him."

"Did Dr. McKinnon tell you that?"

"He said Billy Ray has pressure on his brain, and they have to operate to relieve it. When I asked him if Billy Ray was going to be all right, he wouldn't say. He said they had put the surgery off as long as they could because it was dangerous, but now they had to take the risk."

Amanda could tell from Kitty's halting explanation that the surgery was a desperate effort to save Billy Ray's life. The next hour would be a critical one for the Johnsons. "Is there anything I can do for you?" she asked in concern.

Kitty began to cry. "I just wish we were back at home with our families. Some of them ought to be with Billy Ray. At least, if we were still at home, we would have the minister come and pray for him."

"There's a chaplain here at the hospital. Would you like me to ask him to come and pray with you?"

Kitty nodded gratefully. "It would help a lot. I guess I'm just about prayed out myself."

Amanda put in a call to the hospital chaplain, who agreed to come at once. But observing the young woman, so tired and worn in her loneliness and fear, Amanda could see that she desperately needed the support of her family. "Don't you think it's time we called your families?" she asked gently. "Shouldn't Billy Ray's parents know what's happening to him?"

"They'll just be all the madder at us." Kitty sobbed miserably. "They told us when we wanted to get married that we were asking for trouble, and Billy Ray's accident proves it. They'll only blame me more when they find out about him."

"Maybe not. And even if they are upset, they

still have a right to know about him. Why don't I call them and tell them what has happened?''

A faint hope stirred in Kitty's eyes. ''Do you think they'd come?''

''Let's at least give them the chance,'' Amanda said. Experience had taught her that it was never possible to predict people's reactions, but at least Kitty would have met her responsibility. Whatever happened, she wouldn't have to live with the burden of the guilt she might later feel if she didn't let Billy Ray's parents know of their son's condition.

When Kitty nodded in agreement, Amanda took down the information she needed to notify the families. As soon as the chaplain arrived, she went to her office to make the telephone calls. By the time she returned, Kitty was much calmer. The chaplain's quiet support had given her the strength she needed.

Amanda was also able to give her good news. ''I talked to both your parents and your husband's parents. They're coming as soon as they can get here.''

''Were they very mad at us?'' Kitty asked fearfully.

''No, but they were terribly concerned. Naturally, they're worried about Billy Ray, but they were very relieved to have found you. They want to be here with you to help however they can.''

"You see, you aren't alone, Kitty," the chaplain said with a reassuring smile.

After the chaplain had gone, Amanda stayed on to offer Kitty what support she could. Her work was finished for the day, and she was free to wait with the anxious young wife for news of her husband. The quiet of the evening had settled over the hospital. Only a few concerned relatives still remained in the lounge, speaking in hushed tones. Time dragged endlessly as they waited for news.

Kitty talked about her life with Billy Ray before his accident. Amanda listened sympathetically to her stories about their life in the small town where they had grown up, keeping her thoughts off the critical work that was going on behind the doors of the operating room.

Kitty's voice trailed away suddenly as the surgery doors swung open. Ross came toward them, accompanied by Rose. Both of them were still attired in surgical garb.

Ross looked tired, but his voice was firm and precise as he spoke to Kitty. "Your husband withstood his surgery well, and we think we've taken care of his trouble. We'll be watching him very closely for the next few hours, of course, but with a little luck he ought to be on his way to recovery."

Kitty burst into tears of relief. "Does that mean Billy Ray's going to be all right?"

Ross permitted himself a faint smile. "Let's just say that at the moment things look good for him."

"He's in the recovery room now, but we'll be taking him back to his room in a little while," Rose explained. "You can wait for him there if you'd like."

Amanda remained in the background while Ross finished his explanation. When she saw Rose move in to assist Kitty, she slipped away quietly. She wasn't needed any longer. The nurses could help Kitty.

As she was leaving, Ross glanced at her, seeming to be surprised when he recognized her. She couldn't tell by his expression whether he approved of her presence. She only noticed that he didn't smile. Nor did she. She nodded perfunctorily and turned away.

Amanda walked slowly to the hospital parking lot. After she got into her car, she paused for a moment before she started her drive home. Darkness had fallen over the city, and its skyline was outlined by a glittering display of lights. There was a loneliness in the anonymity of the night. And yet she drove home with a feeling of satisfaction. Perhaps the Johnsons could now look toward happier days. Billy Ray was over his crisis, and their families would soon be here to help them. From here on, they should be able to manage on their own.

Chapter Thirteen

Life settled into a predictable pattern. Amanda's workday routine was interrupted only by the usual problems of her job, and her personal affairs were uneventful. The recent disruptions to her life had ended, and her days were harmonious once again. Too harmonious. Her life lacked vibrancy.

It was all because of Ross, of course. As short as their relationship had been, it was magic for Amanda. She couldn't forget her joy at being with him, the special understanding they had shared. Nor could she get over her pain at the loss of his friendship. And yet it was over, and she had to accept the fact. Her time with him had been a brief, enchanted interlude that wouldn't come again.

She had seen nothing of him. He was once again

lost in his surgical labyrinth, detached from the other business of the hospital. While she continued to be assigned to his patients, she had no contact with him. He sent his nurse as his representative to the rehab staff meetings that concerned his patients. The papers Amanda sent to his office were signed and returned promptly, but without comment. He seemed to have vanished into the hospital complex.

She told herself it was just as well. If she was not to be a part of his world, she needed to separate herself from it. She needed to heal.

Even more mystifying was Tony's silence. While he had seemed sincere in his offer of friendship, Amanda had heard nothing from him since the evening at the polo club. Connie reported that he was now totally committed to his program of therapy and devoted every minute of their sessions to his treatment, never mentioning his private life.

Nor had there been any word from Erica. Her interest in Amanda and Connie had faded now that she no longer needed their help. This was, of course, the way it should be. The therapists' reward came in seeing a patient return to former interests. It was a tribute to their success when they faded into the past and were no longer needed.

It was entirely unexpected, then, when Dr. Foster made an announcement concerning Tony at a rehab staff meeting. "You'll be reading about this in the newspapers very soon, and I wanted you to hear the details from me. Tony Lawrence has made an endowment to the hospital establishing a special treatment program for spinal-cord injuries. A dedication ceremony will be held soon, and he particularly wants the members of his rehabilitation staff to be present.''

Amanda turned to Connie in surprise. ''Did you hear anything about this?''

''Not a word.'' Connie's eyes brightened with enthusiasm. ''What a wonderful thing for Tony to do. Just think of all the people who will be helped.''

''I think we're just discovering what a really fine person Tony is,'' Amanda said.

She left the meeting, deeply gratified by Tony's successful rehabilitation. He had only needed a push in the right direction to show him how to redirect his life. Maybe his accident would serve as a blessing in the long run, not only to him personally but also to the many others who would benefit from his generosity.

Later on the same day, she learned that Tony wasn't the only patient to be blessed. She was working at her desk when she looked up to see two middle-aged women coming toward her desk. One of them was holding Beejee, Billy Ray and Kitty Johnson's son.

Amanda rose from her desk and went to meet

them. "You must be Beejee's relatives," she said, smiling.

"We're his grandmothers," the two women said in unison.

"And you've certainly got a grandson to be proud of. All of us here at the hospital have fallen in love with Beejee." Amanda reached out to pat the baby's arm. As she held out her hand to him, his chubby fist closed around it, and he stared up at her with round, inquisitive eyes.

"You've all been mighty good to him—and to Billy Ray and Kitty. We can never thank you enough for what you've done for them," one of the women answered. Noting her dark hair and blue eyes so like Kitty's, Amanda immediately identified her as Kitty's mother.

"And for us," Mrs. Johnson said. She strongly resembled Billy Ray. "We've worried ourselves sick about these kids, wondering where they were and how they were managing. As terrible as it was the day you called us about Billy Ray's accident, we're so glad to have found them."

"They were just frightened," Amanda said. "And too proud to admit they were having trouble managing on their own. Sooner or later, you would have heard from them. They missed their families and all their friends at home."

"They're going to get some kind of welcome from everybody back home too," Mrs. Johnson said. "We're taking them home with us tomorrow when Billy Ray is released from the hospital. There's going to be a big party for them at the church next weekend. Dr. McKinnon says it won't hurt Billy Ray to go."

"I understand he's going to recover fully," Amanda said.

"Dr. McKinnon says he'll be as good as new once he gets his strength back. Of course, we'll be bringing him back here for checkups. We want Billy Ray to have the finest treatment, and Dr. McKinnon is the best," Mrs. Johnson said.

Kitty's mother nodded in enthusiastic agreement. "He saved that boy's life."

"Dr. McKinnon is a fine surgeon," Amanda agreed.

"We know how lucky we are to be taking Billy Ray home after that terrible accident. We're going to see that the kids get all the help they need from here on." Mrs. Johnson leaned over to plant a fond kiss on Beejee's cheek. "Not to mention this little fellow. You can bet he's going to get plenty of attention."

And plenty of love, Amanda thought as she watched the two proud grandmothers leave the office with their grandson. The Johnson family was definitely headed for happier times if their parents had anything to say about it.

She resumed her work with a sense of satisfaction. People like Billy Ray Johnson were what her work was all about. Successes like these made the troubles, disagreements, and disappointments worthwhile. The problems and sadness her work so often brought were more than compensated for by the reward of seeing people returned to happy, productive lives.

Another success was celebrated when the dedication ceremony for the City Medical Center Spinal Injury Foundation was held. All the staff members of Social Services attended. Significantly, the endowment did not bear Tony Lawrence's name.

The occasion was also noticeably understated, with only a few hospital officials, doctors, and staff members on hand. At Tony's request, there was no fanfare accompanying the event and only a discreet announcement in the local newspaper.

Tony attended the ceremony, accompanied by Erica. They made a handsome couple as they stood together. Wearing a gold-colored wool suit that set off her bright, coppery hair, Erica complemented Tony, with his dashing, athletic good looks. Now completely recovered from his accident, he looked tanned and fit.

After the hospital representatives finished their speeches of acceptance and thanks, Tony spoke briefly to the people assembled. ''As all of you know, I was recently a patient at this hospital. If it weren't for the skill and dedication of the doctors and staff members at City Medical Center, I wouldn't be standing here today. I particularly want to express my thanks to Dr. Ross McKinnon, Dr. Ian Foster, and the members of my rehabilitation team who, with their patience and commitment, made a major contribution to my recovery. This project is dedicated to them.''

When Tony finished speaking, he reached for Erica's hand. The two of them passed through the assembled group of people, speaking to each of them personally. When they stopped beside Connie and Amanda, Erica offered them a special smile. ''What can we say to the two of you after all you've done for Tony? A simple thank you would never be enough. The only thing we could think of was to give you these.''

Reaching into her handbag, she took out two envelopes and handed them to Connie and Amanda. ''These are passes to the polo matches—for each of you and a guest. The seats are in Tony's box so you'll be sitting with us. Tony and I hope you'll use them as often as you can.''

''You may see more of us than you want to,'' Connie said. ''You've made polo fans of both Amanda and me.''

''All the better. Now that Tony won't be coming in regularly for therapy, we had to figure out a way to make sure we'd see you. You've become very special to us.''

"As a matter of fact, I'm not sure I could manage without you around to nag me on a regular basis," Tony said to Connie with a grin.

She responded with a raised eyebrow. "Thanks—I think."

He laughed and turned to Amanda. "As for you, I want you to know that I've found out what a devious woman you are, and there's something I want to say to you about it." There was a glint of mischief in his eyes as he bent down to whisper in her ear, "This isn't the time or place, of course. I'm saving it until we can be alone."

For a moment, Amanda was taken aback by Tony's words until she saw that he and Erica were smiling at each other conspiratorially. "I'm afraid you haven't heard the last of him," Erica warned. "He has some very special plans for you."

"Then maybe you'd better tell me about them," Amanda said to Tony, now curious.

He shook his head. "Later—at the proper time when I can tell you in a proper way. I like suspense."

"This I've got to hear," Connie said. But Tony and Erica had moved on to speak to Dr. Foster, leaving them mystified.

"I'm not sure I want to know what Tony has on

his mind," Amanda said doubtfully. "His surprises usually turn out to be pretty disruptive."

"But always interesting," Connie reminded her.

The conversation moved on to other subjects then as other staff members joined them to talk excitedly about the impact of the new project. As they chatted, Amanda's glance strayed across the room to Ross, who stood with a group of doctors. Unexpectedly, her eyes met his, and she saw that he was watching her steadily. She looked away quickly without acknowledging him, but a pang of regret tugged at her heart. It still hurt to see him and think of what might have been.

But then she reminded herself that she was only indulging in wishful thinking. There had never been any real hope of anything meaningful between them. Their worlds were too far apart. There had been only her foolish, impossible dreams.

She turned her attention back to her coworkers, determinedly ignoring Ross's presence. When the reception broke up a short time later, she hurried to leave the room.

As she moved toward the door, she saw with surprise that Ross was standing in her path. There was a questioning look in his eyes as she came toward him. "Amanda?" he said, seeming to want to speak to her.

She nodded at him politely, but she passed by without speaking. There was nothing she wanted to say to him. Ross had given her enough grief already.

It was later in the afternoon when Amanda looked up from her desk to see Tony and Erica coming toward her. Both of them smiled broadly.

"I know we've taken a long time getting here, but there were a lot of things that we needed to settle," Erica began. "Both of us agreed that we didn't want to see you until we had everything worked out."

"I'm sure there was a lot of work involved in putting the spinal-injury project together," Amanda said, understanding. "It really is a wonderful thing you're doing, Tony."

He brushed aside her thanks. "It's been a pleasure, and we plan to do all we can to assure its success. But the project isn't what we want to talk to you about. We've been making some other, very important plans. Plans that include you." He looked at Erica. "Do you want to do the honors?"

"You go first. You're the one who's mainly responsible." She smiled at Amanda. "I want to save my part until last."

Amanda's curiosity was now thoroughly aroused. "This all sounds very mysterious."

"Up until this moment, it has been. You're the first to hear the news." Tony pulled Erica close to him and slid his arm around her shoulders. "We wanted to wait until my therapy was a success and the arrangements for the spinal-cord foundation had been worked out. But now that both have been accomplished, I'd like to announce that this fantastic woman has agreed to marry me.''

"Oh, Tony, I couldn't be happier for you!" Amanda cried out in delight. "I knew when I first met her that she was perfect for you."

A twinkle of amusement sparkled in his eyes. "As a matter of fact, she told me about that first meeting. From the moment you two got together, I didn't have a chance. The two of you would have made an upstanding, responsible man of me no matter what I tried to do."

"Are you sorry?" Erica teased. "You can still change your mind, you know."

"Never. Now that I've seen the error of my irresponsible ways, I'll never return to them." He hugged her tightly. "Besides, I could never manage without you. I'd not only be totally miserable but I couldn't possibly carry out all my plans without you to help me."

"What plans?" Amanda asked.

"First, we're going to build a house at the farm. My other interests can be run just as well from there while we go about the much more enjoyable business of raising horses—polo ponies for me and thoroughbreds for Erica. We plan to do some traveling with our horses, of course. Erica wants to enter some of her thoroughbreds in hunter-jumper shows, and I want to keep my polo ponies in action. Strictly as a spectator,'' he added quickly.

"All this will take place after the wedding. I've got most of the plans made,'' Erica said, her eyes sparkling. "The ceremony will be at the hospital chapel with only a few special people in attendance, but we'll have a huge reception at the Polo Club afterward. The only thing I've got left to do is ask those few special people I want to be in the wedding. I'm asking you first, Amanda, because it's likely there wouldn't be any wedding if it hadn't been for you.''

"I doubt that. Tony is a smart guy. He would have figured it out eventually,'' Amanda said with a fond smile.

"But look how much time I might have wasted,'' Tony objected. "And there's been enough wasted already.''

"Since we certainly don't want to waste any more, the wedding will be very soon,'' Erica added. "That is, if you'll agree to be in it, Amanda. I'd like you to be my maid of honor, and I plan to ask Connie to be a bridesmaid.''

Amanda accepted the invitation with pleasure. "I'm honored, and I'm sure that Connie will be too.''

"If all goes as planned, it should be only a matter of days,'' Erica said in excitement. "Just wait till you see the dresses I've picked out. They'll be beautiful on you and Connie. I thought turquoise for you, to match those wonderful eyes, and yellow, to complement Connie's dark hair. Of course, if you don't like what I've chosen, we'll change them for something that pleases you. I want this to be a perfect occasion—for everyone.''

She launched into an ecstatic description of the plans she had made. Tony stood by, looking pleased and proud. He finally interrupted with a question. ''Do you suppose all this could wait until after we've spoken to Connie? Besides, you ought to leave a few surprises for the wedding day.''

''He's right, of course. I don't want to spoil things.'' She smiled indulgently as Tony took her hand. Before she turned away, she said softly to Amanda, ''Thanks so much for everything. You'll always be very special to Tony and me.''

Amanda watched them leave. The glow of their happiness lingered after they had gone. These two generous people, who had made this such an important day for so many others, deserved all the happiness life could bring them.

It was almost dusk when Amanda parked in front of her apartment house. As she approached the apartment door in the semidarkness, key in hand, she didn't see the obstruction in her path until she had stumbled over it.

She looked down to see a lanky figure sitting on the sidewalk, propped against the wall beside the door. Leaning closer, she saw that it was Ross.

"I've been waiting for you, Mandy," he said. "I seem to be in big trouble."

Chapter Fourteen

Amanda regarded Ross indignantly. "What are you doing sitting here in the dark? You could cause a person to kill herself."

He pulled himself to his feet and brushed the dust from his clothes. "I wanted to see you."

"I can't possibly imagine why."

"I've got something I want to say to you. But I can see I'm going to have trouble getting you to listen." Even in the darkness, she could see his contrite expression. "Can I come inside?"

She hesitated. She had spent long nights agonizing over Ross and had only just begun to deal with her injured feelings. She definitely didn't need any more grief from him. "I don't think so," she said, hardening her resolve. "We really don't have anything to say to each other."

"But we do. At least *I* do." His voice was pleading. "Please. Let me say what I've come to say. Then if you want to run me off, I'll go quietly."

It was the forlorn droop of his shoulders that swayed her. Humility was definitely out of character for this man, so much so that it was impossible for her to refuse him. She unlocked the door and signaled him to follow her.

When she had switched on the lamp beside the sofa, she turned to him reproachfully. "Okay, I'll listen—as long as you don't get on my case again. You've given me a hard enough time at the hospital already."

"I know. That's what I came to tell you. I want to apologize. I'm really sorry about the way I've acted—blaming you for things you haven't done and giving you a hard time when you're only trying to do your job. I had everything all wrong. I thought. . . . That is. . . ." His voice faltered and he searched for words. When Amanda's stony regard did not soften, he plunged in again. "It's just that Tony was always hanging around you, and I thought you had something going with him. I didn't know until today—when he showed up with that other woman . . ."

". . . that Tony wasn't interested in me?" Amanda finished for him.

"When Ian told me Tony was setting up the endowment fund, I realized that I had been wrong about him. Then when I found out that he had given up polo and was working hard on his recovery, I knew the story about him in the newspaper had to be false."

"I tried to tell you so, but you wouldn't listen," Amanda reminded him.

"But I thought you had a thing for Tony. What else was I to think when I saw that picture of the two of you holding hands?"

"You could have let me explain," Amanda said, unmoved.

"I was too steamed to think straight. But when Tony came in today with that other woman. . . ." His voice trailed away, and he looked at her penitently.

"While we're at it," she said, "we might as well get the facts straight. Tony and Erica are getting married. They're going to live at Tony's horse farm and raise horses, and he's not going to drive race cars or play polo anymore. He knows how fortunate he is both to have recovered from his accident and to have Erica. They're perfectly suited to each other, and I know they're going to be happy."

"But Tony was always making moves on you, and I thought. . . ."

"Then you ought to have known better. Tony

was a sick man. As a doctor, you know that sick men do strange things.''

''So do jealous men,'' Ross said unhappily. ''All I saw was this good-looking millionaire hanging around you. And I was jealous. I admit it. What man wouldn't feel threatened by Tony Lawrence?''

''A man who was openminded enough to listen to another person's side of things.'' Amanda leveled a reproachful glance at him. ''A man who trusted that person's word.''

He ran a hand through his hair in distress, rumpling it further. ''Don't make me feel any worse than I already do. I know I acted like a fool.''

She brushed aside his explanation. ''It's over and done with now, and there's nothing to be gained by dwelling on past misunderstandings. I accept your apology and hope that we'll be able to work together better in the future. That is, if you have no objection to working with me.''

He groaned. ''I wasn't concerned about our working together. You know I think you're the best.''

''I didn't exactly get that impression.''

''I acted the way I did only because I was ticked off about Tony. You're a psychologist—you ought to know better than anybody what jealousy can cause a guy to do.''

''Jealousy didn't have anything to do with the

way you dumped me after we went fishing,''
Amanda said, her anger erupting.

"Dumped you? What are you talking about? I
called you all day Sunday, and you were out. You
left town on Monday without saying a word to me,
and when I finally found out you were back in town
and came over here to see you, I found you cuddled
up with Tony.''

"I was not!" Amanda exclaimed with a resentful
glare.

"That's the way it looked to me," he said grudgingly.

"But you obviously don't look at things the way
other people do. If you had really wanted to talk
to me, you could have called me Sunday night."

"I was in surgery. A former patient's son wiped
out on the freeway, and the father wanted me to
take care of him. Then when I called you Monday
afternoon, you were gone—without telling me.''

"I didn't know I was going to the conference
until I got to work that morning.''

"You could have left me a message," he accused.

"I didn't think you'd want your desk cluttered
up with personal messages. Besides, you didn't
leave me a message when *you* found out *I* was out
of town.''

"By then I was beginning to wonder whether
you'd want to hear from me. I thought maybe I

had come on a little too strong and you'd had second thoughts about us, so I decided to wait until you got back into town to find out what was going on.'' He looked at her unhappily. ''Then I came over here to find you with *him*.''

''I had no idea he was coming. I was terribly disappointed that he was here when you came. I wanted to see you and find out if—if—'' Her voice faltered, and she swallowed hard. ''When you acted the way you did, I thought you didn't want to see me again.''

To her dismay, her eyes suddenly filled with tears. As she struggled to blink them back, Ross exclaimed unhappily, ''Don't look at me like that. Don't you know the last thing I would ever do is hurt you?''

Her lips quivered in spite of her effort to control herself. ''You didn't act like it.''

''That's because I'm stupid. All I wanted was to be with you.'' He held out his arms, and somehow Amanda found herself melting into them. As his embrace tightened around her, she rested her head against his broad shoulder, loving the feel of his cheek against hers as he murmured to her softly, ''I didn't know how to tell you, Mandy. After all, with an exciting guy like Tony to choose from, why would you want to spend your time with a dull, uninteresting doctor like me who has to spend most of his time shut away at a hospital?''

"You're not dull," Amanda said. "You're impatient and demanding and sometimes utterly insufferable, but definitely not uninteresting."

He grinned. "Does that mean you love me?"

"You're tempting me."

"Then let's work on it. Given enough time, I think I can convince you."

His lips found hers in a long, sweet kiss, and Amanda was lost in a glorious whirl of feelings. Somehow she found herself sitting beside him on the sofa, nestled in his arms.

Neither of them heard the key turn in the lock. Only when the door opened and Connie came into the room did they become aware that they were no longer alone.

Connie's eyes widened, but she gave no sign that she noticed Amanda's flushed cheeks or Ross's rumpled hair. "Hi, Amanda. Hi, Ross," she said with a grin as she passed through the room and went on to her bedroom without looking back.

Ross leveled a suspicious glance at Amanda. "Does this sort of thing go on around here all the time?"

Amanda pulled away from him in indignation. "You have a distrustful mind."

"Where you're concerned, I'm paranoid," he said, drawing her back to him. Holding her close, he pressed his cheek to hers and murmured, "I guess I'm a fool about you. I don't think very straight when I'm around you. I'm sorry about everything. I was so confused—all I knew was that I was falling in love with you. Mandy, I want to share my life with you—forever.''

When he pulled her back into his arms and his lips found hers once again, she discovered that she wasn't thinking very clearly, either. But then her arms slid around his neck, and she quit trying to think at all as she gave herself up to his kiss and the joy of loving and being loved.

Suddenly they became aware of a steady beeping. ''Ross, I think your pager is going off,'' she finally said.

He sighed in disappointment as he rose from the sofa. ''I guess I'd better call the hospital.''

Amanda smoothed her mussed hair while he made his telephone call. He turned away from the phone a short time later. ''I've got to get back to the hospital, but I don't think I'll be very long. Maybe we could still get in a late supper at Kovac's.'' His eyes were pleading as he added, ''That is, if you're willing to wait for me.''

But Amanda knew that he was already distracted by the emergency that awaited him at the hospital. It would always be this way with him. Brilliant, dedicated to the people he had pledged to help, Ross would always put his duty as a doctor first.

And it was all right, she knew with sudden clarity. He wouldn't be the man she loved if he were any different. He had taken on the responsibility of caring for other people; what he needed was someone to care for him. And she knew that she could be happy being that person, that she could find fulfillment in helping him. After all, wasn't helping people what she had committed herself to?

"It's all right. Go on and do what you have to," she said with an understanding smile. "When you finish at the hospital, I'll be there waiting."